The Big Round

The Big Round
a novel

Linton Baldwin

Spuyten Duyvil
New York City

Copyright © 1954, 1995 by Linton Baldwin

Published by Spuyten Duyvil
P.O. Box 1852
Cathedral Station
New York, NY 10025
(212) 978-3353

The Big Round was originally published by Lion Books under the title *Sinners' Game*. *The Big Round* is the original title of the book, though, and SD requested that the author use his own title rather than the one selected by the pulp fiction publisher who first brought it out. Nothing in the text has been changed.

First Spuyten Duyvil Printing

Printed in the United States of America

ISBN 1-881471-08-X, hardcover; 1-881471-09-8, paperback

 Produced at The Print Center., Inc., 225 Varick St., New York, NY 10014, a non-profit facility for literary and arts-related publications. (212) 206-8465

for Karen,
this time around...
thanks for being around

Introduction

The first time I met Linton Baldwin I was struck by his rumpled elegance—that he wore a suit and tie and was possessed of this casual formality, almost a throwback to another time. His suit looked expensive but it also looked as if he had been sleeping in it. The second thing I learned about him when we became friends was that he was not only a gentleman but also a sportsman. Naturally his sports were ancient, formal ones, too: tennis and boxing.

For many years he has lived in an apartment across from the Central Park Wildlife Conservation Society (you know, the zoo), but he's more likely to be found, not so much on Fifth Avenue, as he would be on the other side of the park, sitting in some luncheonette, talking to a retired counterman about the best horse to bet that day at Belmont or playing tennis later in the day at the River Club or going to theatre with his girlfriend or having dinner with some old big-band bandleader or a childhood friend. Sometimes, early in the morning, he's in the Opera Espresso across from Lincoln Center, arguing betting lines with his old friend Frank Hammond, the mammoth-sized former tennis umpire who used to get into fights with John McEnroe. Occasionally, even I am there, soaking up all this atmosphere and sports information.

Like the author William Burroughs, Linton has a penchant for wearing suits with a tie—and a pair of sneakers. In the case of Mr. Burroughs, it was—no, not Nike's, even though he appears in their commercials now, but hightop Converse's—and in Mr. Baldwin's case, it was a pair of black lowtop Mephisto's. Both writers also came from privileged backgrounds, but also were familiar with—one might even say preferred—the seamier details of life. Believe me, it is sheer delight to walk through Times Square with Linton Baldwin, not only because he knows the theatre world and its people, but he's likewise familiar with the bookies, addicts, ladies of the night, con artists, alkies and street poets. He once gave me a wonderful essay he wrote on meeting Jack Johnson in a Times Square side show, a detail of which, alas, has gone from the Deuce (42nd Street).

Born (1926) and bred in Brooklyn, he ran cross-country and played tennis at Brooklyn Poly Prep, and at one time was the number one ranked Eastern Junior Doubles player along with partner Bill Tully. Lint's father was a friend of Eddie Eagan, the World War One heavyweight champion in the military and former Olympic athlete, and he grew up in a household playing tennis with people like Gene Tunney, the professional heavyweight champion who beat the mythical Jack Dempsey. He had the good fortune to be a copy boy at the Daily Mirror when Dan Parker, the unofficial dean of boxing, held center stage at that newspaper.

Baldwin came of age during the Second World War and served in the U.S. Marines in the waning days of that conflict. Later, he attended Yale where he became the first freshman to play the number one slot on the varsity tennis squad; and he eventually became the captain of the varsity cross-country team. One of his friends, a schoolmate and fellow jock, eventually became the President of the United States (George Bush). After college Baldwin worked in television, radio and advertising, and wrote scripts in Hollywood, but he never strayed far from his two loves—tennis and boxing. *The Big Round* (formerly *Sinners' Game*) was published in 1954, and later in the Fifties Lint worked for what eventually became Sports Illustrated.

His friends include people like the late tennis great Bill Tilden and the professional tough-guy Lawrence Tierney ("Reservoir Dogs" and the title role in "Dillinger"). Tilden was Lint's tennis instructor; he met Tierney when the actor was down on his luck and driving hansom cabs in Central Park for a living. He's also been profiled by the great journalist, Lillian Ross, in a recent tennis magazine article. And he's led an active life in New York professional theatre, investing in Broadway and off-Broadway productions.

Besides being a gentleman and a sport, Linton Baldwin likes to make friendly wagers and is, like James Boswell in another time and city, a denizen of the night. But through much of these activities, Baldwin mostly has been a writer, and all of these experiences shape the narrative of his short, subtly written novel, *The Big Round*.

Once, in Clarke's Bar, the great welterweight fighter Irish Billy Graham told Baldwin that he had read the novel and liked it. Lint, at first skeptical that Billy had read his book, finally became convinced when Graham—who said he had been in training to fight Chico Vejar when he read Lint's novel—quoted from the text. And, of course, Graham is one of the few fighters from that era who actually gets mentioned in the story, too.

Nowadays Baldwin spends a lot of time at sporting events and the theatre, two of my own favorite places in the world, particularly boxing matches and off-Broadway plays. In that sense, he and I see eye-to-eye on lots of issues, which is how we got to know each other and become friends. Essentially we both view the world in dramatic terms. Yet I am not writing this introduction simply because Lint Baldwin is my friend; I am writing it because this is a wonderful novel that is full of the rhythm of boxing from a time when boxing was at its greatest moment.

You can breeze through this book in a few hours, just the way you might read any pulp fiction novel, as a way to pass the time. But you also can read this book carefully as I would recommend you do, noting the way the author bends a phrase or word here and there. You also can re-read this book, something that can't be said for too many novels at any time. I recommend that you read *The Big Round* slowly and carefully, then re-read it several more times.

Picture my friend Linton, too, in his expensive, rumpled suits, always wearing a tie, looking world-weary but never uncivil, full of urbanity and charm. Like William Burroughs, he's the one also wearing sneakers. Though he doesn't smoke or drink anymore, still try to imagine the odor of cigars and whiskey, french fries and nickel beers. This big round was served up by one of the last gentlemen, this odd combination of F. Scott Fitzgerald and Damon Runyon, both of whose ghosts fit neatly into the world of *The Big Round*. It's a book written by one of the nicest, most generous people I know, and these qualities, while not literary values, shine through on every page of this book. Read it and imagine yourself hanging out in one of those morning luncheonettes on Broadway with that marvelous character—Lint Baldwin.

—**Michael Stephens**

One

"Why, your Royal Highness, I should have no objection to fight the whole regiment, only be kind enough to allow me a breakfast between each battle."
                              —JACK BROUGHTON

THE FIRST TIME I saw Johnny London I knew he had it—everything, that's all. He could hit. Christ, he could hit! Harder than any light-heavy I ever saw in my life. That takes in about forty years of watching 'em come and go, but when the good ones start to go I try to be somewhere else.

It was a Saturday afternoon at Stillman's, a gym on New York's Eighth Avenue where you can see, smell, hear, and feel the only thing in the world for unhappy guys like me.

It was a hot day in July. Most of the boys were watching the first ring on the left as you come in. Petey Vincenzo was trying to show them, and himself, that he hadn't left everything he ever had under the Arizona sun. He'd been baking out there for three years.

"It's your only chance to live," the doctors told him when he left. It was said they were telling him the same thing now, but he was back. Friday night he planned to make us all know he was as good as ever. He was matched against a kid from the lower east side who hadn't been off his feet in twenty-eight starts.

I was watching him too, and hardly noticing the couple of boys pulling themselves up into the other ring. I'd seen Petey when he was a promising young welter who didn't have reason to be afraid of anyone. Now I found myself wishing to hell he'd be afraid of this kid from the east side and go back to Arizona. Unless someone had arranged otherwise, he was liable to be hurt very bad within six days. From what I'd heard, nobody had arranged otherwise—and I usually heard, even now.

Then, all of a sudden, I didn't give a damn about Petey Vincenzo, or anyone, or anything else except me and Johnny London—though I didn't even know his name then—and the kind of dream you wouldn't know anything about. There he was in the other ring, awkward as they come, but doing things naturally that you try six, seven, eight years to teach a fighter to do at all. They had to be natural, because a lot of the things he did were so awkward you would have had to laugh at them. We did—months later when we talked about them and they were gone. There was the sloppy way he flicked with his left, the way he telegraphed some of his punches, and some of the stances he took would have done for those Police Gazette cuts you see of old timers like Charley Mitchell, Jake Kilrain, and John L. I never saw a fighter do so much good and so much bad at the same time. He was working with a good, tough boy named Hall who'd been doing time here as a sparring partner for two, three years. I'd seen him give plenty experienced heavies and light-heavies all they could ask for in the way of workouts and never once get in real trouble. He knew how to take care of himself.

Then Johnny threw that right. I came halfway out of the rickety chair I'd planned to spend the rest of the afternoon in. I knew right then my plans were changed for that afternoon and probably for the rest of my life. Hall's knees were sagging, the one eye I could see over Johnny's right shoulder was glazed, and his arms were at his sides, helpless. He was as out on his feet as a guy can be. Johnny's back muscles stood out as he kept Hall from coming apart all over the ring. He was faking at working in close and doing a good job of it. Hall's a tough boy and he came around fast. In a few moments the two were working easy again.

When the buzzer ended the round, I cased the room. I'd seen that right hand land and what it had done. I knew what it meant, or could mean to me—and Johnny. There were three, maybe four other guys in the room who probably would have grabbed up the big meal ticket when it was shoved at them. If one of them saw what I saw I was in for trouble. If all of them saw, I didn't have a chance—or, that's what I thought. But that was before I met Johnny London, the only fighter I was never able to blow up. He was that good.

Gino Martell was still munching on his cigar and watching Vincenzo's feet. He'd know where to put his money Friday night by watching those feet. He'd never know about the something real big he missed. Frank Moriarity just sent a kid over to the concession stand for a beer, a thing he'd not be doing if he got the scent. The two other guys I worried about were having a joke together. They hated each other's guts, so it must have been some joke.

Hall and the kid stopped boxing. They were taking off their head guards. The kid was smiling, handsome like, a little like Billy Conn. He was saying something funny to Hall. Hall was smiling, too, and shaking his head from side to side, as if to clear it, only in fun. He should have been thanking Johnny for not knocking it off, I thought. Maybe he was.

The two of them climbed out of the ring and started back toward the lockers. I wasn't sure how to play it. If I stopped the kid and talked to him right now somebody was bound to notice.

Sometimes I wish I was born with a big friendly mouth. This was one of the times. But I wasn't, and at Stillman's they knew it. If Ben Hackett talked to anybody, it was for a reason and with a purpose. I think most of them knew it wasn't a matter of being unfriendly or anything like that. It was just a matter of rearing, along with the sureness that the time was running out fast. Nobody knew more about the two big strikes on Ben Hackett than me.

"You're Ben Hackett, aren't you?"

The kid took it out of my hands. He was standing right behind me. When he spoke I whiffed the smell of his sweat and heard the easy way he was breathing. From that day on you could have struck me blind and pushed me into Johnny's corner or a room where he was being rubbed down and I would've known he was there.

"Yeah, I'm Ben Hackett. That's a nice right. Much experience?"

"I have a left, too. And I can take a punch. Army experience, that's all. A guy in Korea—you wouldn't know him—told me to look you up." He waited.

"Meet me at Walker's, down the street, when you're dressed; I'll be at a booth."

He turned and left. I waited a moment and then walked over to the concession counter. I bought a pack of cigarettes, and sauntered outside.

I went down to Walker's and slid into an empty booth. I was on my second beer when Johnny came in the door. I motioned to him and he came over and sat down opposite me.

I'd seen the important things in the ring at Stillman's. Still, there were other things I had to find out about the greatest piece of raw fighter I'd ever seen. There were plenty of little things that could be the matter to keep us from going anywhere.

I decided to feel him out. "Why don't you do yourself a favor, kid," I asked him, "and find an easier way to make a buck than fighting? You're still young. How the hell old are you anyway?"

His eyes bore into me. "I'm twenty. I'll make more money fighting than I can any other way. I'll make it fast. I think I'll make it faster with you."

"How about your family? What do they think?"

I guess I must've asked every boy I ever worked with since Georgie Knize about his family. I still wake up nights sweating, hearing that crazy, fat old woman yelling at me— "barterer in human flesh," that was her label for me.

"My mother's dead. My father lives in California. He doesn't know where I am and wouldn't care. I just got here from California."

It was good so far.

"How about broads and booze? You might as well level with me now. We don't want a misunderstanding—any time."

"I don't drink. I'll have a beer when I like, that's all. I don't have time or money for women. I don't like the kind I find down here. Maybe when I'm at the top, all the way..."

"How long have you been in New York?"

"Three days."

"Where are you living?"

"Up there." He jerked his thumb towards uptown. "In the park. I just got a job as a counterman in a place a couple of blocks over. I can probably get a room tonight." I didn't think they came that way any more—a hungry fighter! And with a punch.

I gave him five bucks and told him to get a room at the 92nd Street 'Y'. I said I'd call him there the next morning. Then I went home to tell Ruth we'd have a new boarder starting Monday.

He was mad at the world.

I thought about it driving home over the Queensborough Bridge that night. Ruth and I were still living in Long Island City. We were in the same neighborhood we'd started out in over twenty years ago—there was never any reason to change.

It was getting dark. Ruth might be worried. I usually got home from my job at the garage between six and seven on Saturdays. Now it was a little after eight. I had walked almost all the day down to Canal Street after talking with Johnny London. Then back over to 59th Street and First Avenue where I'd parked Joe's car. That's Ruth's brother. He loaned the car to me on Saturdays because he was usually working. All in all, he'd been awful good to us. He was still working for the same company where we'd first met. We were working together as armed guards. Only difference was now he was a supervisor and making enough money to send four kids to school. He wasn't toting a gun any more and didn't wear a uniform. He sat behind a desk and made sure the new men in the company got there in time with their uniforms and guns. It was pretty soft. I guess if I'd stuck with the company it would have been a desk for me too. If Joe thought I wasn't doing right by Ruth he never said so. I think maybe she asked him to but he never did. Maybe he figured it was none of his business. Maybe just by being a fight fan himself he had some idea of my sickness. I doubt if he could know what it was really like. I think you'd have to have it awhile to know that. Maybe he had an idea.

Every good fighter I ever knew started out because he was sore at something or somebody. Sometimes the being sore can be so bad it ruins a fighter. Maybe I'd have thought it was that bad with Johnny if I'd only talked to him. I thought how lucky it was I'd seen him in action. If he'd just come up to me and started talking I don't know what I'd have done. I've seen fighters with a lot less of those feelings in them who couldn't do a thing once they got in the ring. Sometimes they just went out of their heads when they got hit. It wouldn't happen with Johnny. It couldn't. He was too cool in there with a big, fast boy like Hall who kept shooting them at him.

I looked at the house before I went up the steps. It was like every other house on the block and the ones on the other side of the street. It wasn't much of a street. There wasn't much paid on the house but it was a lot nicer to come home to than the crummy apartments we'd lived in around there. The real estate guy who sold it to us would be sorry to hear I was going to quit my job. It would most likely mean the next payment would be late. I tried to set him straight on this before we bought it—tried to tell him about my way of living, so he'd know why when the payments were late. It didn't seem to bother him then. Maybe he thought I was kidding—or was coming near the time when I'd 'settle down.' Maybe Ruth got him aside and told him everything would be O.K., that he'd always get his dough on time. I don't know. I know he always got sore when he didn't get it on time.

The house was quiet when I let myself in. I thought maybe Ruth went down to a movie. She likes them and goes a lot. I turned on the hall light and went in the parlor. She was sitting in a big chair by the window, asleep, breathing hard. I went over and bent down to kiss her. I would have got the story quicker but I had a cold.

It only started a couple of years before. It didn't figure to be much to worry about at first. In the last year it had got a lot worse. She'd been putting away about a bottle a day for that time. Even by the hall light I could see a lot of what it did to her. There was still a lot of the old beauty there. There were a million lines, too, that weren't there a short time ago. There was a puffiness coming to her cheeks. They used to curve in once, so graceful and thin, that I worried maybe she'd get TB or something. The clean white skin that was one time pulled so tight over the bones was becoming blotchy and slack. I loved her—then and now. It was my fault she started—I knew that. There wasn't much reason to stay beautiful for a guy who quits his job and takes off to look for something as soon as he gets just far enough ahead to pay the rent and grocery bill for a couple of weeks or months. I never gave her the clothes or helped us meet the kind of friends that might make a woman try to look nice. If I could bring home a winner this time maybe I could make some of it up to her. It all depended on a twenty-year-old kid I'd met that afternoon.

I sat down on the arm of the chair beside her. I put one arm around her shoulder and took one of her hands with the other. She didn't move. She was really under. I sat there with her that way for about ten minutes. I tried to wake her gentle with some pressure at times on her hand or shoulder. I said, "Ruth, wake up, I'm home," a couple of times but nothing happened. I went into the kitchen and made some coffee. When I came back into the parlor she was in the middle of a yawn, and then she was mumbling something in her sleep. It made me sick and sore at both of us to see her like this. I began to shake her, a little rough, and brought her around.

"Ruth, come out of it. It's me. C'mon, baby, it's Saturday night. Let's get on the town. Whadda you say?"

"Sure, sure... let's get on the town. Swell. Big time. You got enough for... a movie? There's a swell one downtown... "

I put the coffee down on the table beside her.

"Take it," I said.

She picked up the cup and saucer with both hands. She lifted them up to a couple of inches from her mouth and brought the cup the rest of the way with one hand. It was shaking pretty bad like I figured it would. Some of the coffee would have spilled sure except that I filled it only halfway. She took a couple of swallows and put it back on the table. She shook her head, closed her eyes, and eased back into the chair, breathing hard. I stood there watching her for about a minute, I thought maybe she'd gone back to sleep.

Then, without opening her eyes, she said, "Will you get me the pills out of the medicine cabinet?"

I went out and brought back the pill bottle with a glass of water. She was leaning forward now with her head in her hands. She looked up. I handed her the bottle without opening it. It was mean and lousy—the way I meant it to be. It was a new bottle and she couldn't get the top off. I watched her struggle with it. All of a sudden I felt worse than I had in a long time.

"Here, gimme that," I said.

I grabbed the bottle away from her and wrenched the top off.

"Hold out your hand."

I dropped three tablets in it. She brought her arm in close to her side and held her wrist with the other. She was shaking that bad. She wouldn't've asked me to help her with the bottle, no matter what. Our life had turned into a whole lot of little dirty things like this. I turned away and walked over to the window. I couldn't take watching her put the pills in her mouth and swallow them. It would be slow and careful. I knew around how long it would be. It happened a lot now. She wasn't good at drinking. When I was sure she had them down I turned around.

"Feel better?"

"I feel all right."

"Why don't we go for a ride or a walk or something? I've got some… news for you."

"Thanks, anyhow. Maybe I'd better take it sitting down. I'm going right to bed. Thanks for coming home so early with all your good news."

"We'd still have time to catch the last feature at RKO."

"Thanks again. Good night."

She started to get up.

"Sit down. How much did you have to drink today?"

"That's none of your damn business. If you want to tell me something, go ahead."

"What the hell do you mean it's none of my business? It's our money, so it's some of my busi—"

She laughed. Not a real laugh. More like just "hah, hah, hah" in words.

"Our money! Don't be ridiculous. You mean your money, don't you? The money you bring home—got any idea how far that would go? Thank God we don't have to depend on it. See? This is my money."

She pulled two twenties from inside her dress. She waved them at me. She stopped and stuffed them away, nervous-like.

"Where'd you get them, Ruth?"

She smiled.

"You'd like to know, wouldn't you? Why don't you try and find out, then?"

She started to get up. I took a couple of steps and stood in front of her so she couldn't.

"I don't need to. You're going to tell me right now."

Then there was a change in her face like she was scared. Sudden-like, she seemed to sober up. I guess she just got the idea she'd let the cat out of the bag about this extra dough.

"Leave me alone, will you, Ben? I'm sick. Can't you see? It's your money, of course. I found a cheaper grocer a few months ago down on—"

"Where'd you get it, Ruth?"

She was lousy at lying—one of the things I loved about her.

"Joe gave it to me. He does sometimes when there's a little left at the end of the month."

I'd had all kinds of dirty thoughts about where she might have got it. I hated them and was sore at myself for having them. That she'd got it from her brother wasn't so bad. There was nothing nice about it either.

"How can Joe have anything left at the end of the month? He's sending four kids to school, isn't he?"

"I don't know. How do you manage to save enough to take off for weeks and months at a time? You cut down on things—everywhere. Somebody has to go without. In your case, it's me. In Joe's, it's the kids—or Margaret, I guess."

"Why should his kids go without? What right have you—"

"What right have I got to take money from my brother? What right have you to let your wife go around in a dress like this? To make us eat the kind of food we do? To make me sit here every night with nothing to do? Not even having television or—"

"We could get a television on the installment plan."

"Oh, stop it! Everything we have is on the installment plan. If you'd just stay at a job we could pay for things. We could have our own car and get a good house... new clothes every so often... eat the kind of food that makes you feel good all the time like you want to go and do things. And then, once in a while, we'd have the money to do them."

I knew the more she went on the tougher it was going to be. I figured I better get it out fast.

"That's the way it's going to be, honey."

"What?" She looked at me like she didn't get it. "What do you mean?"

"I mean the tough days are just about over for us—I think. I'm sure. It'll take a few months—maybe close to a year. After that it's gonna be a new kind of life for us. We'll dump this house and get a swell one out in the country. But we won't stay there all the time—not on your life! We'll come into New York two, three, maybe four times a week and see shows and stuff. And you'll have the right clothes to wear, too."

She looked real happy. "Ben, I don't want to see two or three shows a week. Maybe sometimes we could see a show. You know I'd rather just stay home with you—if it was a nice home. One we could be proud to just come into and have friends in sometimes.

Wouldn't you like that? And me looking pretty in a good dress when they come in. And being able to have something nice cooked up for them, and some wine, the red kind, and—"

"We'll have it whatever way you want it." I cut her off sharp. Sudden-like I was sick of talking about it. I was going to bring home a winner. That was the big thing. The other stuff, and more, would come with it, always does. I wanted that stuff, sure. That was part of it. But now wasn't the time for thinking about it. Now was the time to start thinking about a twenty-year-old mind and body—how to take care of it, make what was good there now even better, and cart off what was bad. That last is always a big order.

"I know you can do it, Ben. It'll seem hard at times. Like when the boss, who doesn't know half as much as you do, starts telling you how to do the job—that sort of thing. But it'll always be all right when you get home. I'll make it so—believe me, please."

"You don't get it, honey." Maybe this was the wrong way to do it. It was my way. "I'm quitting my job Monday. I found a fighter I've been looking for at Stillman's this afternoon."

"You—you found—"

The look on her face made me feel lousier than I had in a long time. She didn't, for a minute even, see what I was getting at. She'd thought I was telling her how I was going to turn over a new leaf, that now I'd decided to stick with a job and help build something.

"You don't really mean it. You can't. Please say it, Ben. You're fooling. You're not going to… "

I was all mixed up with being sorry for her and being sore about the way she was taking it.

"I'm not fooling, Ruth. I saw a boy today who's got enough natural stuff to be the best in the light-heavies—with the right handling. I know I can bring him all the way up. He's only twenty, probably still growing. He may be big and heavy enough to lick anybody in a couple of years."

"But you've tried before—so often. So many fighters you felt you could make into champions… and always there turns out to be something wrong with them. It'll be the same way again, I know it. You know it."

I sat down in a chair on the other side of the room. Just before telling her I was going to quit my job, I'd felt edgy. My stomach was working overtime. For just a couple of seconds there when she wasn't getting what I was trying to tell her, I felt like I didn't have the guts to go through with it. Now it was O.K. It was out

19

and clear. I figured she knew nothing could change me.

Then she said it: "Ben, if you do this, I'm leaving you."

She meant it. I'd expected her to say it a lot of times before—more as a threat. She never did. She wasn't doing it like that now. She must've been thinking about it a long time. It came to me then how big a part of me she still had. I got a feeling of a coming loneliness that was like nothing I ever had before. Even all the times I'd been away from her, traveling around, I was always sure she'd be there when I got back. I guess just then it hit me what a really good feeling it was.

"You wouldn't do it, Ruth. Not now, when our big chance is here."

"I will, Ben, believe me. I can't take it any more. I can't take seeing you come back again some day, maybe two, three months from now... that beaten look on your face... and knowing that this one's let you down somewhere, that the boy's head or jaw wasn't hard enough, that he cried when he got hit. I don't know. They all let you down somehow. And then comes that period when we're climbing back again. I get scared to open the door for fear it's another bill collector. We're behind on the house and they're telling us how sorry they'd be to have to turn us out on the street. No, thanks! I think almost anything would be better than having to go through that again."

I was thinking fast now. I was feeling a lot of things I didn't know I had left in me to feel. A lot of good things had piled up in the years of living together. Sure, most of the excitement was gone. Anyhow, it was for me. There were times, though, especially lately, when I wondered about Ruth. She seemed to want to do things we'd never done before. I thought maybe it was on account of the drinking. It was only a couple of times and I knew she'd had a few. I didn't have any and was pretty much all in from working both nights. Tried talking about it later but Ruth didn't want to or was too busy. She was always funny about talking about anything like that. I felt kind of good about her being that way. There were other times too when I think it would've helped to talk.

It seemed like life without Ruth wouldn't be worth the trouble. If she left me, I didn't think I'd even have enough life left in me to make my bid with Johnny. If there was just some way...

"I need you, kid." I don't say stuff like that good or easy. "Trust me this once, will you? I know we've got a winner this time. I never said that before; you know it. I might've said I thought a boy looked good in the gym, that he had a nice left hook—things like that. But I never told you I had a kid who I was sure could make it in the big time. This one can. I know it, Ruth. It'll mean getting the things you—both of us—want, and fast. Like I said, with a little luck, in a year or so—"

"Stop it, Ben!" It was a kind of half-scream. "Stop it! It's the same thing, the same story exactly. You talk about me drinking. You're worse, much worse. You're like the worst kind of drunk when you get this way... when you see a fighter who you think may... have it. I don't know enough about it, but I think... you see some boy doing a thing the way you did it when you were fighting... when you were winning forty straight and thought you were on your way to the top. You think, because he does this one thing, that he'll have the rest of it, or you'll be able to teach it to him. You shut everything else out. Part of your brain closes up. You won't see anything else but this one thing."

"Ruth. I promise." I said it like I was throwing in the towel. In a way I was. "It'll be the last time. I promise you. If we don't make it this time there won't be any more tries. Is that good enough for you? Please—for both of us—go with me this one last time, will you?"

"No. I'm sorry, Ben."

She got up and left the room. She went into the hall and I heard the bedroom door close. I went out in the kitchen. I put some ice and ginger ale in a glass and came back to sit down and try and figure where I was. I didn't think I'd go as far as I did, saying I'd give the whole thing up for good if I didn't turn the trick with Johnny. Even that wasn't good enough for her. I tried to think what it would be like, bringing him along and getting there and not having Ruth to share it with. It seemed like it wouldn't be so good. Maybe I'd feel different after a few weeks or months. I didn't think so.

I sat there, it must have been an hour. Once it sounded like Ruth was making a phone call in the other room. I wasn't sure, not until the doorbell rang and I went to answer it and saw Joe. She'd called him, asked him to talk to me. I'm usually glad to see Joe. I didn't show it this time. It figured to be a worse night than I expected.

"Can I come in, Ben?"

"You know you can, Joe—any time. Do you have to get in the middle of this?"

"I don't want to. Thought maybe I could help out some way. Let's go down to Case's. We'll have a brew. O.K.?"

Joe's been too good to us over the years for me to give him the cold shoulder. I didn't want to hear any speeches about what a lousy husband I'd been for his sister all these years and why didn't I start making up for it now. I knew all about it. Nobody needed to tell me.

I should have known Joe better than that. When we had the brews in front of us, he asked, "How much are you going to need?" I was set for chit-chat or maybe the buildup to the speech.

"I don't get you, Joe."

"Ruth says you've got a fighter you're sure you can make champ. You haven't been at this last job long enough to put away very much. You're going to need some dough at the start before he starts winning. How much?"

"I don't know; a hell of a lot more than I've got."

"Where will you get it?" So he was trying to talk me out of it this way, was he?

"It won't work, Joe. Don't try. I'll get enough, somehow. Even if I have to go into hock for the rest of my life, I'm going to have this last shot."

I got up to start to go.

"Sit down. Don't you get me at all? I'm with you a hundred percent, Ben. I'm trying to help."

I'd heard something like that about twice before in my life when I was sure it was on the level. You hear it dozens of times from guys like Gino Martell. You know they're trying to get you in a corner every time.

"Thanks, Joe." What else can you say? Then I said, "How come, Joe?"

"How... how come what? Oh. Well, I don't know. I guess maybe because I've never taken a real chance in my life. I think I'm about due. Ruth told me everything you said about this new boy you've found... that you're sure he can win. You're never said that before. I believe you. I know more about boxing than you think. Enough to tell that you know your stuff. I'm thinking maybe sis is going to get the stuff she's been deserving all her life. If it happens fast it won't be too late. This is the only way it could happen like that. I'm thinking maybe you're going to let me and Margaret and the kids in on the jackpot—whatever part you say— nothing on paper. It's my kind of investment."

"Sure, you'll have a piece of Johnny... and he will win. We'll all be living high soon. But... didn't Ruth tell you she'd leave me if I went ahead with this?"

"I talked to her a long time on the phone. I told her I was sure you meant everything you said—about quitting if you missed this

time. You meant it, didn't you?"
"She's my girl, Joe. Maybe it don't always seem that way from the life I've given her. If that's the way she wants it…"
"That's the way it's got to be, Ben."
We sat there at Case's for a while. It was a big thing for Joe. With my rep, borrowing something here and there wouldn't make a bit of difference. With Joe, I knew it added up to a lot more. Like he said, he never borrowed a dime in his life before. There were times when he was pretty hard up and could've used a few. After a bit we got to talking about how much it would take to get going. It was going to be done right. Johnny London wasn't going to fight until I knew he was ready. He was going to have all the right stuff while he was getting ready. I could see by Joe's face after a while that he didn't know it would take anything like what we were getting to. He most likely figured I'd saved a little more by now than I had. He took it O.K., didn't say a word. He's not the kind of guy to back out on you. By the end of the night we'd got it all down pretty clear. Too clear, in a way. Johnny had to win a couple of real big ones anyhow or we'd be trying to dig our way out of the hole for the rest of our lives.

There was only one way to work it. I'd had it figured when I left Johnny on Saturday. He was going to eat right, and he was going to have the right place to live in. Our place. It was small, only one floor, but it had a small extra room we didn't use. It had a bed in it and a desk. There was a time when Ruth and I had hoped to have a real need of that room. I remember one time when we were both awful excited, a little scared too. We'd been married about three years. Ruth was about four weeks past her time. We were all set to ask Joe and Margaret if they were planning to use their crib in about nine months. We'd almost forgotten that Ruth was sick with the flu a little while before that. It was pretty bad—most likely the reason she was so late. When we found we were wrong and wouldn't need the crib, neither of us knew how to act. We both sort of made as if we were happy about it. I was, in a way. We sure weren't ready for anything like that. If we'd known it wasn't going to happen again after that—at all—I guess we wouldn't have been happy at all.

I was sitting there thinking about it when Ruth walked in. She'd brought me some tea and toast.
"Is it all right with you if Johnny London stays with us—in the extra room? He's only twenty, never been in New York before. He could get in a lot of trouble most places."

She stood there a couple of seconds like she was saying the words back in her head. She started to say something and stopped. Then she said, "It's all right with me, Ben."

It sounded funny, almost like she'd got beat at something. She went out and I got back to work.

I guess I got all the figures down pretty straight. When Joe looked them over later he said they made sense to him. I could see even better when I got it all down on paper that I couldn't have made it this time without Joe's help. I'd used up too much credit the last time out. Ruth didn't want to hear any of the talk about it. She went in the bedroom when we started on it. It only took us about an hour to get it all squared away. Joe never once talked about backing off, but when we were winding things up I saw it was bothering him again—the way we were getting in real deep. I gave it to him then as close as I could about Johnny—the way I saw him at Stillman's, how he'd taken everything out of Hall with that right hand, the way he moved—the whole business, fast. I couldn't even fake telling him the way Johnny looked so good to me. He got something of the picture anyhow. When he left he was like a guy who's swiped the family savings to put on a sure thing.

"What room you got Johnny London in?" I asked the desk guy at the 'Y' Monday morning.

He went back to one of those boxes where they keep mail and keys. He took a piece of paper out of one of them.

"You Ben Hackett?"

"Yeah, that's right."

He put a key down on the desk in front of me.

"He went out. Said he'd be back in a couple of hours. That was an hour and a half ago. You can wait in his room. Four-twelve."

I went up and waited. It was about the smallest room I'd ever been in. A bureau, a bed, and a chair covered almost all the floor. I felt better when I saw his beat—up little bag sticking out from under the bed. I'd forgotten to call him Sunday what with all the figuring and the business with Ruth and Joe. I got a funny feeling when the guy downstairs said he was out. Maybe he got a ride back to California. Maybe he decided he could get by working full time as a counterman—and come away a lot less scratched up. Maybe he just chalked it up as the easiest fiver he ever made and took off. Still, the bag was there. He could buy two or three new ones like that with five bucks. On the bureau there was a comb with some teeth missing. That and the bag were the only things around that told somebody'd been there. That didn't say he was coming back. I opened the top drawer of the bureau. There was a picture in it. Not a photo—one that was painted. It was good. It was of a small island somewhere. There was water around it and the sun was out. The water looked real and the sun looked warm. I was starting to take it out of the drawer to look at it better when the door opened. It was Johnny.

"What the hell are you doing?"

"Trying to figure out if I was wasting my time here. Thought maybe you'd skipped."

"With your five?"

"Yeah, that's right."

He pulled three bucks out of his pocket and threw it down on the bed.

"Keep it. I spent the rest."

"How'll you pay for the room?"

"I won't."

"You could get arrested."

"They let you out after a while."

I sat down on the bed and lit a cigarette. He was still standing there with the door open.

"Sit down," I said.

"Why?"

"I thought you said you wanted me to manage you—something about making a lot of money fast."

"That was before you went in that drawer. Why'd you have to do that?"

"I told you—thought you might have taken a powder on me. Didn't want to waste my time hanging around—not if you weren't coming back."

He shut the door slowly. Then came over and shut the drawer with the picture in it. He ran some water in the basin that was next to the bureau and sloshed his head and face in it.

"Some girl give it to you?"

"What?"

He turned off the water and grabbed a small towel off the rack.

"The picture," I said. "Where'd you get it?"

"I painted it—a place in Korea I looked at a lot... every day for almost sixteen months."

He sat down on the chair.

"You gotta know everything about me, don't you?"

"That's right—everything. I got a lot involved."

"So have I."

"All right. Why talk about it? Where you been?"

"Running around the reservoir."

25

"A couple of hours? You always run that much?"

"Yeah. More, a lot. I stopped early—figured you might be waiting."

"Uhhuh. Look, are you gonna do what I say—all the time?"

"That's why I came from California."

"You came all the way to see me? There are managers out there. Why didn't you look up one of them?"

"A buddy in Korea told me to look you up—said you were the best. He'd seen you do great with boys who had a little. Said he knew you could make me champ."

"Who was this guy?"

"Name was Ed, that's all I know."

I scowled at him. "What do you mean, that's all you know? You came across the country to get me to take you on, because some guy named Ed told you I know my stuff? Am I supposed to swallow that?" Christ knows I wanted to.

"I don't care whether you swallow it or not, Mr. Hackett—except that I want you to manage me. Why the hell would I lie to you?"

I couldn't figure an answer for that.

"We were in a foxhole together two days and nights. It was the only time I saw him. He'd seen me box in the interservice matches in Japan a little while before. He was older than me—maybe forty. We talked about everything. Got to know each other pretty well. He was a boxer himself at one time. He never worked with you. He met you once in Chicago—said you wouldn't remember. Told me all about what happened there and how you got a rough deal on the whole business. He knew what he was talking about—I could tell. We were cut off together all that time—the Reds everywhere around us. It looked like we'd get out O.K. when he got hit. One of the Reds was behind our lines, wounded. They thought he was dead—he wasn't far from it. Anyhow, he figured he'd take Ed with him. Then I got hit—not bad, but just enough to knock me out for a couple of days. When I came to, nobody was able to tell me anything about Ed—his whole name, nothing. I guess maybe if I'd worked on it I could've found out. He didn't have a family or anybody he would have wanted me to see. I would've messed something like that anyhow."

A million faces came back out of the years in Chicago. There were a few Eds. None of them would be about forty and none of them would have been caught in Korea—they were too smart. It looked like this one did a hell of a lot more for me than any of the ones I remembered.

26

"Who taught you to fight like you do?"

"I had an uncle who taught me how to hold my hands when I was a kid, that's all. He thought it would be good for me to know."

"You like it in New York?"

"How the hell could anybody?"

I did. That didn't mean I saw how anybody else could.

"You're gonna stay at my house with me and my wife awhile. I'll want to keep an eye on you all the time—at least while we're starting out. O.K. with you?"

"Sure, it's O.K. with me. Sounds like you're making a full-time job out of it."

"That's the idea."

He smiled for the second time since I'd seen him. The teeth were good—white and even. Except for the nose that had taken a few hard ones, you'd never figure he'd done some fighting.

"All right," I said. "You got anything in that bag?"

"Yeah. I got everything in it."

"Grab it and let's get out of here."

He took the picture out of the drawer and put it in the bag.

We grabbed a bus at the corner of Lexington Avenue going downtown. It was crowded. We had to stand up going down to 42nd Street. At 42nd Street we were edging our way, slow-like, up to the front, so's to get off. A couple of people had got in between us. There was a big woman in a dotted dress moving along in front of me and behind Johnny. There were four people between Johnny and the side door. The woman began to push past him. He came around fast, like she'd goosed him. The woman almost went down, it was so quick. She was thrown against a woman behind her and a couple of packages began to bounce around the floor.

"Keep your hands off me," Johnny snarled at the woman. She was red and spluttering and plenty scared. She didn't say anything to Johnny, wouldn't even look his way. She looked once. It was enough. I swear to Christ I never saw anything like it. It was the kind of look that told you he just wanted to hit something—it didn't much matter what. It could've been the toughest guy that walked—or a woman. He wanted, more than anything, a reason to start belting. Quick-like, I stepped past the woman and grabbed Johnny by the arm. I half pulled, half pushed him out the door.

"I'm all right. What are you—"

"Keep walking, kid. Simmer down."

We walked about a block before I said anything.

27

"Let's have some coffee."

We went into a Horn and Hardart's and got the coffee and sat down at a table against the wall.

"What was it all about?" I asked.

"I don't like to have people touch me. I don't like to be pushed. I was moving ahead. She was going to get out all right. There was no reason for her—"

"I don't like it either, kid. But, you know, for all the people in it, it's a small city. You just can't help that kinda thing once in a while."

"I can help it. I can make 'em stop—like I did her."

"You're likely to be around New York a long time, Johnny. Especially if you get close to the jackpot. You think it's worth it?"

"Sure it's worth it. When I'm making dough I won't be riding in buses."

We drank our coffee while I wondered if I'd bit off more than I could chew.

"You wear that stuff all the way from California?"

"Yeah."

He'd washed them a few times, he said. Probably one more wash and they'd come to pieces for good.

"We got to get you some others. C'mon."

We walked a couple of blocks over to my old tailor's. He did a good job and didn't take your leg. I hadn't seen him in a long time. It was a while since I bought a new suit.

"Hello, Mr. Hackett!"

I never knew a tailor who didn't have a memory like an elephant.

"Hello, Harry. How you been?"

"Pretty good, Mr. Hackett. What can I do for you?"

"Not a thing for me, Harry. You can fix up my boy here with something good."

It was a long time since I'd called a fighter "my boy" like that.

"Sure thing, Mr. Hackett. He gonna be a champ?"

"We think so, Harry. He can hit."

Harry gets a lot of good suits turned into him that have been made for other guys. Sometimes they make a deposit on them and then don't show up to get them after they have been made. Sometimes they don't look the way the guys thought they would and they don't want to wear them. After about ten minutes of looking, Harry came up with a blue one like that. You could see it was never worn before. It fitted Johnny pretty good the way it was. Just trying it on made Johnny feel a lot better. You could see it right away. Harry said he could have it ready by the end of the week. He never had anything ready for me in less than two weeks. He must have seen the change it made in Johnny, too. I told Harry we'd pay him when we got the suit. It was O.K. with him. I 'd given him a couple of good tips in the past. He knew if Johnny won a few we'd both be back after that. And we wouldn't be getting suits that were made for other guys.

"Thanks," said Johnny when we got outside.

"For what?"

"For the suit."

"A champ's got to dress like one, don't he? Listen, you're gonna be buyin' me a couple of suits a week—twice as good as that one—in a while. You'll be payin' for the stuff my old lady's always wanted too. Sure, I'm gonna help, but if you don't deliver, it's no soap."

I know managers who tell their boys ninety times a day he's nothing without them, that he couldn't fight his way out of a bag without them in his corner pulling the strings. A lot have gone pretty far that way. I'm yet to see a great one brought along like that. I figured Johnny for maybe—great. For that he had to have the big feeling every great one has. Conceit. Yeah, that's it, conceit, pure and simple. Not self-confidence or anything like it. Any of the great ones knows what it feels like. Some of them had it in the beginning. Others had to get it along the way. They're not so nice after that. But it's great when you see it happen.

It seemed like maybe his walk was a little different when we got out—a kind of swagger to it. His face looked more relaxed. We were walking east when he spotted one of those out-of-town newsstands.

"Hey, wait a minute. Maybe I can get an Altadena paper."

I walked over with him. He spotted one down near the bottom of the rack. He took it out. He was leafing through it when this guy poked his head out from behind the stand.

"Whadda you want?" the guy asked.

"Just want to see if this has the coast ball scores."

"This ain't no lendin' library fella."

Johnny put the paper under one arm. He reached in his pants pocket and pulled out a dime. The guy behind the counter got a kind of half-smile on. Johnny put the dime on the stand in front of him. When the guy reached for it, Johnny tore the paper in half and threw it in his face. There was another guy standing there and he laughed. The guy behind the stand swore at Johnny and reached down and under. He came out from behind the stand by a

29

door in the side. He had a piece of lead pipe in his hand. He started for Johnny.

"I'll fix you, you fresh punk!" he said.

He saw I was with Johnny. He had his eye on me, too. As soon as it started I was ready to jump in.

"Come any closer with that thing and I'll kill you."

Johnny wanted the guy to come closer—you could tell. There were about twenty people standing around. A whole bunch more watched from across the street. You never see them come so fast as they do in New York when they smell blood. There was the guy who always yells "break it up!" and the others who shout him down with "let 'em fight!" Johnny and the guy just stood there glaring at each other. Johnny was crouched, ready, and sticking his chin out at the guy. Somebody said, "Here come the cops!" There were a couple of them coming fast down the block.

"Lucky for you, punk," the guy said.

"The hell with you! C'mon, you still got time."

The guy didn't move. The cops got there. One grabbed Johnny the other two grabbed the guy. One of them took away the lead pipe.

"What were you going to do with this?" asked the cop.

The guy was drooling now, he was sore.

"Get him, that's what. He tried to wreck my stand."

"All right, kid. What happened?" the cop holding Johnny asked.

"I was looking at that paper—" Johnny pointed to the half of it that fell on the street "—to see if it had my hometown ball scores in it. This stupid bastard asked me if I was in a lending library. I paid for his paper and gave it back to him."

"So you came after him with this?" asked the cop, holding the lead pipe.

"Can't you see he's a nut? It was self-defense," the news guy said.

The cop took another look at Johnny. You never saw anybody look easier. It was like he was apart from the whole thing—just looking on.

"We could run you in for littering the streets," the cop told Johnny.

"I guess you could."

The cop held the lead pipe for another gander. It was a mean-looking thing. Johnny most likely would've been too tough and fast for him, but I was glad the guy turned chicken.

"You can claim this at headquarters tomorrow if you want it," the cop told him. He turned to us. "You better buy your paper someplace else from now on," he said.

That was that.

Walking on over to the subway I tried to figure it. There was the chance the newsstand guy was right—maybe I had a nut on my hands. Sure, he was mad at the world. But so were a lot of other guys who didn't show it like this.

"You ever been in jail, Johnny?"

"A couple of times."

"Why?"

"Things like that, nothing much."

"You can't win the title sitting around in the cooler, you know."

"I know. Don't worry, I can stop. I got a reason for stopping now."

"You had the same reason a few minutes ago. It didn't stop you."

He didn't say anything for about half a block.

"Why do people act like that? Why do they talk that way? Is there something wrong with me that makes them want to give me the business? It happens all the time."

"Don't talk like a jerk," I sometimes wish I could get things over like a doc or a preacher, soft all the time. "That bastard would of been the same to anybody. He's got troubles too."

Johnny shook his head. He didn't go for it. "No, it wouldn't've happened to anybody but me."

When we got home Ruth was out shopping. There was a message from Joe that everything was going good. I showed Johnny his room.

"It's a little bigger than the one at the 'Y'. The bed's a lot softer than any they got in the park."

"It looks good."

"Take it easy a while. You look like you can use some sleep. I got some work to do."

He pushed off his sneakers and flopped down on the bed. I went in the other room to do some more figuring. I wanted to make a couple of calls, too.

I called Barney Ellis out in Jersey. Barney started with just one tourist cabin out there. It wasn't long before he had a couple of them. Next thing anybody knew he had a regular little tourist court. He never knew much about real estate. He knew nice country when he saw it. Pretty soon he found he could make more dough by turning the place into a pint-size resort. Each year he kept building it up a little more. One year he put in a tennis court.

31

A couple of years later he was able to afford a swell little swimming pool. It went on like that. Then one year Paddy Markle, who lived out near there, was getting ready to defend his middleweight title. He decided Barney's would be a great place to train. Barney was all for it. He's always been a fight fan and he was especially a big fan of Paddy's. Trouble was getting a ring. They don't come cheap. Paddy was so eager to stay out there near home that he loaned Barney part of the dough to get the ring. Barney was able to talk an outfit that makes rings into letting him put that part of the dough down on it and paying the rest later. He didn't have an idea that he'd be able to pay the whole works off as soon as he did. It seems everybody wanted to see Paddy work out—he's always been a popular, colorful guy, giving a big show both in the ring and out. They came from all over to watch him. Then a lot of them, once they got there, decided to stay at the resort for a couple of days. It's only about forty minutes over the George Washington Bridge, real easy to get to.

Then Paddy won his fight and pretty soon there were other guys out there training, and Barney had to keep on building.

When I got Barney on the phone, I came right to the point. Told him what a good thing I had in Johnny, that I was flat, and needed a place to work with him. There was no beating around on his part either. He said he'd carry me long enough to see if the boy was as good as I thought. He knew if the kid shaped up, it was likely to turn into a good long—term thing for him, from a lot of angles. I said we'd be out the next day.

I was just hanging up when Ruth came in with the groceries in her arms. I jumped up to give her a hand.

"Honey, we're on our way! Everything's falling in place. Barney Ellis is going to let us work out at his joint—on the cuff, until Johnny starts to pay off. It's the perfect set up—fresh air, swell country for roadwork, a chance to keep an eye on him all the time so's guys like Gino Martell can't get to him. There are bound to be plenty of good boys for him to work with there and—"

"Tell me about it later, Ben. I'm tired."

"Sure, kid."

It wasn't part of the deal for her to get behind the thing. She was on her way out to the kitchen when Johnny walked in. He'd washed up and put on one of my shirts. Ruth stopped at the kitchen door.

"Hi, Johnny!"

She said gay and loud—and phony.

"Mrs. Hackett?"

"That's right. Very good. He thinks fast, Ben. Ben tells me you think even faster in the ring. Is that so?"

"Maybe."

"It better be so. You're supposed to drive a big gravy train for a lot of people. You know that, don't you?"

"As long as I get my share, it's O.K. with me."

I didn't like the way it was going. I tried to step in.

"C'mon, you two. Let's quit the jockeying. We're in this thing together."

"Jockeying? I didn't hear any jockeying. Did you, Johnny?"

"No, not a thing."

She walked right over to him and took his hands in hers. He looked down at her, with her bending over them, close.

"They look strong. What happened to this one?"

On the left one there was a small ridge running along behind the knuckles.

"That's the last thing my father ever gave me. I was reaching for an extra potato. The doc didn't do much of a job fixing it."

Ruth touched it lightly with her fingertips.

"It doesn't hurt?"

"Good as new—for hitting. Just looks kind of funny. Most people don't notice it. You're the first in a long time."

She let his hands go. "Aren't you afraid of cuts and wounds, Johnny?"

"They heal."

"Sure they do, Johnny… we all do. Good luck—for all of us."

It was a lot more than I counted on. It was a start.

Two

"Please don't stop it, Mr. Donovan. I won't bleed any more."
—Henry Armstrong

JOHNNY LONDON was on his way like an express train when he first saw the girl named Rain. Rain Ellis, Barney's daughter, twenty-five, blue eyes in a face like an angel, and a figure that shouldn't have been let loose around a fight camp.

It was about three o'clock in the afternoon. Johnny was working with a kid named Lenny. On my orders the kid was throwing a couple hundred lefts per round at Johnny. Johnny's next go figured to be his toughest. We'd taken seven straight, but we'd yet to run into a left hook like Billy Patrick's. Lenny was getting Johnny ready for it. When the last round ended I was pretty sure we had it made. Johnny went four rounds with four different partners that day, and he looked better in each one of them.

He was stepping through the ropes onto the ring apron when he spotted Rain. She was sitting there on the grass in a white tennis outfit that looked like it was made special for her. Maybe it was. There was nothing that Barney wouldn't do for her. That's why it always made me so sick to think of the things I knew about her. Not 'things,' really. The one thing. I figured Barney would try to kill anybody who went to tell him about it. There was a time when I think I would've too. I knew her when she was just a kid and a sweeter one you couldn't find.

She was sketching on a large drawing pad. Johnny threw on his red-and white-striped robe and came over to have a look. He was standing right behind her, watching her work. He could've been a thousand miles away for all the attention she paid.

"Jesus! You're going to put some clothes on me, aren't you?" he asked.

The picture was him, all right. I had to admit it was a good job. It could've gone on a poster and you would've known it was him. Only it couldn't've gone on a poster the way it was—with no trunks, no nothing.

She looked up, surprised and smiling. She had the kind of teeth you only see in magazine ads. She made a couple more swipes at the page and then held it out in front of her with both hands. Johnny looked at the picture and at the smooth brown of her arms with the soft light hair on top.

"Do you like it?"

"Pretty well. But the right arm... did you... "

"Oh, nuts, you can tell, too! I've been trying so long to get it right. I just don't know what I'm doing wrong. I didn't think it was so bad, though, that you'd notice."

"You mean just being a fighter and all?"

"No, that's not what I mean. Why do people always... " He bent down beside her and reached for the pencil. "May I?" She handed him the pencil. He made some short, careful swipes at the pad while she held it in her lap.

"There. You see now what the trouble was?"

She looked at him, amazed.

"I do. Thank you. I'll begin the whole thing over tomorrow. I think it could be quite good now."

"See you."

Johnny was starting toward the path heading up to the clubhouse when she jumped to her feet. Every move she made was easy and graceful. It wasn't hard to see how she'd gotten in a couple of Broadway shows. Just chorus stuff, I heard, but still...

"Johnny!"

He stopped on the old dime.

"Would you pose for me sometime? I mean for a real painting? You could be on the wall in the Modern Museum."

"Thanks, anyhow. The wall of the Garden's good enough for me."

"Well, then, at least you can have dinner with us tonight. They have a new band at the resort this evening. It's supposed to be wonderful. At least, Dad says they'd better be—for the money he's paying them."

"Dad? You're Barney Ellis' daughter?"

"That's right. Yesterday was the last day of the term at school and I'm home for the summer."

"Home? You mean here—for the summer?"

"Now, you're not going to be one of those, are you? You don't believe a training camp is just no place for a girl, do you?"

"I didn't... well, now that you mention it, I think you have a point."

"Oh, you do! Well, that's too bad, because this summer I expect to be around more than ever. Of course I live at the resort and usually spend most of my time over there. Right now, though, I'm bucking for my master's degree in sociology and I plan to nail it down with a thesis on the subject 'Pugilistica, U.S.A.' Because of Dad, I've been around fighting and fighters quite a lot. I think I've got sort of a headstart on the subject."

"You'll find some great case studies around here. If you ever

35

need to know anything about me, just ask Ben Hackett. I think he knows twice as much about me as I do."

"I'd rather get the data first-hand—if it's all right with you. Somehow, I don't think Mr. Hackett would care to contribute toward any project of mine."

I looked up from where I'd been making notes on the next day's routine.

"Hey, Ben, what did you do to scare the lady?"

"How's that?" I put away my notes and walked over to them. I nodded shortly at Rain. "Miss Ellis," I said.

"Mr. Hackett. How are you? Now doesn't that sound silly? You know, Johnny, your mentor here has known me since I was a little girl. Then it was always 'Rain-honey,' 'Rain-sweet,' 'how's my little princess?'—he was the nicest man. But sometime since then I grew up—at least, for Mr. Hackett. Now it's always Miss Ellis—my elegant surname. Tell me, Mr. Hackett, when did I grow up for you? Please, I'm really interested."

"I couldn't rightly say. Somewhere along the line, with the high heels, lipstick, permanents, and—like that."

Maybe if I'd come right out with it then it would've been a lot better—it couldn't have been worse. But there was no reason for it.

"High heels, lipstick, permanents—hell! It was something more than that and you know it. Someday you're going to tell me, too. Well, no matter... I've asked Johnny if he'd care to join Father and me for dinner. I know how you probably feel about letting him out of your sight at such a crucial period, so may I extend the invitation to you as well?"

"That's real nice of you. Ruth, my wife, kind of expected us back in town for dinner, I'm afraid. Thanks, anyhow. Johnny, you better get dressed. You'll catch cold standing around like this. Excuse me, will you?"

I started up for the clubhouse, expecting Johnny to be right with me. He stayed, talking to her for a couple of seconds, and then came jogging along.

"Ben, I'm gonna stay and have dinner. They'll probably have an extra room at the clubhouse, so I can stay overnight. If they don't, Rain said she'd drive me back to town in her car—O.K.?"

"The hell it's O.K.! They're all jammed up at the clubhouse this week. Barney told me yesterday, because I thought maybe we'd stay over the weekend. I'll be damned if I'll have you driving with that crazy dame. I've seen her drive and—"

"Why do you have it in for her?"

I could have told him why. I could have told him right then and

36

there that she was no good. They got names for girls like that. And I should have told Johnny about Rain—about her and a guy named Gino Martell. And about the pictures. And God knows how much more there was that I didn't even know about.

Instead all I said was, "Look, I just don't want you breaking your neck at this stage of the game. Is that so hard to figure?"

"For Christ's sake, Ben, nobody's asked me to have dinner with them since... I can't remember. I haven't eaten with anybody but you and Ruth since—"

"Sorry. We didn't mean to—"

"Hell, you know what I mean. Sure, I'm grateful. If I weren't eating with you, chances are I wouldn't be eating—for sure not three meals a day, like now. But if I want to talk to somebody else once in a while, especially somebody who looks like—"

"Don't let that angel face fool you. If you had any idea—all right, kid. If you feel you've got to have some social life we'll have dinner with them. Ruth doesn't expect us, anyhow. She's going over to Joe's for dinner tonight."

"You just said... "

"That's right—because I don't want to go. If you're set on it, tell her I'll call Ruth and explain."

"Sure."

He jogged back down the path to tell her. They were still talking and laughing together when I went in the clubhouse to have a drink.

"You've got yourself a champ this time, Ben. He's getting there fast, ought to stay there a long time. I haven't seen a right hand like that since Berlenbach's."

Barney Ellis knew more about fighting than any guy I knew who never fought. It was a pleasure talking with him again after all the years. Dinner was good and he hadn't paid the band too much. They were good. I'd just about stopped worrying about the girl. A couple of jolts before dinner helped.

I said, "It was the first thing I saw—the right. It looked like he moved good, too. I never thought he'd come along as fast as he did. I swear, it looks to me now like he moves almost as good as Rosey when he was hitting his stride. Honest, Barney, I'm not seeing things that ain't there yet, am I?"

"You're not seeing a thing ain't already there, Bengy. I'd bet on him tomorrow against Price except for—well, you know as well as I do."

I knew. I didn't think it stood out like that, though. It only cost us the KO once. The other time the ref stopped it in the next round.

"You been watching him close," I said.

"Every round for dough. Most of 'em out here, too. Been making it pay off."

Barney had seen the Watts fight. That was the night Johnny got Watts in the eighth with a solid right. Everybody in the house saw it. All he needed to do was push Watts with it again—or even the left—but right away! So what's he do? He steps back, like he's waiting for him to fall right then. It looked like he was expecting the ref to stop the fight. Whatever it was, when Watts didn't fall and the ref didn't stop it, Watts was still just sitting up there waiting for the clincher. So what's Johnny do? He starts pounding away at the gut and lets Watts tie him up in a clinch 'til the round ends. Of course there's nobody better at bringing a guy around than that little Harry Miller who was working in Watts' corner that night. So? So we lose the K.O. It hadn't showed up in Johnny's first couple of starts. Then he was so bottled-up, eager, and scared, that he'd go in like a windmill and keep belting 'til there was nothing left to belt. Once he got those first ones behind him something changed. He was ten times a better boxer now than he was then. Sure, he still wanted to win. He wasn't bottled up any more— leastways not half as much as when I took him on. I wasn't even scared to ride on buses with him. He knew he was paying his way now and he was good. Where before, there was this crazy thing in him, kept him punching automatic-like, now he was confident, poised, thinking the thing out all the way, keeping it in hand. All that was fine, except maybe it had something to do with the way he wasn't finishing them the way he should.

Barney said, "You know, Ben, a lot of the boys used to think maybe Charles' heart had something to do with the way he slowed down when the action started. It couldn't be anything like that could it? Jesus, if it was anything like that... "

I felt cold all over. I thought for a minute I was going to hit the deck. I couldn't even hold the glass. I put it down. My eyes closed. All the Chicago stories came running back to me. There were a thousand guesses why it happened. One doc said one thing, another was off on another trail. X-rays and stuff weren't much then, so they never did get together on anything. Every sportswriter in town became a doc overnight. They came up with some real lulus on the thing. About the only thing they got together on was who was to blame. There was no kicking that around...

It was 1925. He was the best boy I had up 'til then, you see, this Georgie Knize. No great natural thing, sure, but he took teaching as good as any of them. Everybody was looking for somebody good enough to make it rough for Mickey Walker, the Toy Bulldog. Mickey had been making other welters look like suckers for about three years now. He'd really taken over and was running the class—almost a one-man show. There didn't seem to be anybody around who could touch him. Maybe Georgie couldn't, either, I wasn't sure. He'd shown me enough in his first two starts that year to make me guess he was ready for Rinaldo, a kid from Chi who was ranked about three in the welters. I signed the match and the papers played it up big. But they didn't play it the way I figured. They were sore! Sore that this local champ, Rinaldo, was being shoved into a bout with an "unknown" when they figured he was ready for a shot at Walker himself. They tore into me, Georgie, and the matchmakers for trying to take money to see a mismatch like that. It was true Georgie had only been fighting pro for two years, but when they started to make cracks about his style I knew they were shooting blind. All our fights up till then had been out of town. If one of those writers were at any of them I'd have spotted him. I can smell a sports-writer a half a mile away.

I'd seen Rinaldo fight and I knew that Georgie was ready for him. He might not take Rinaldo, but he'd make a good scrap of it. He'd help his rep plenty by going the route with a guy as good as Rinaldo. That's what I thought before the papers took off on us. But then—I'd seen those guys work too often before. Nothing but coming up with a decision or a K.O. would help us now. Anything else would just prove them right. If we lost a squeaker they'd make it sound like the kid never had a chance and was pasted all over the ring.

Most times I try to keep a boy away from the stuff that goes into print. This time I let Georgie know what they were trying to do to us. I let him read the stuff where they said he didn't have a thing, and where did we come off shoving an inexperienced, nothing—talent punk in with a classy operator like Rinaldo? Letting Georgie know did what I hoped it would—it got him sore. Sore in the right way. Not blind, stupid sore so he'd run into the first good combination coming his way. Sore in the way of a kid who's got enough tough ones under his belt to know he's got a right to be called a fighter.

And then that woman came! Fat, red-necked, waddling, dirty, scared. Five hundred miles she'd come from a little town in South Dakota with her husband and Georgie's brother and sister. All to keep her son from becoming a world champion—and me from everything I've ever wanted before or since.

In the middle of the night she came, four days before the fight, and carrying on nutty-like. I wondered if she'd been on this jag for all five hundred miles. Right up to the hotel room Georgie and I were sharing she came with the whole family. The room was filled with them, all crying and shouting, but mostly this one fat old woman. Georgie was telling her to take it easy and sit down. I could see it happening to him right away. Things were going out of him that I'd been putting in since the first day I saw him in that club fight three years ago. She was shouting about religion and how she hadn't raised him to try to kill another boy with his fists. Soon she had Georgie crying and I wanted to throw the whole bunch of them out the window.

"Now, wait a minute, Mrs. Knize. Your son has the most important fight of his life coming up Friday night. It's his big chance. This is no way to be talking to him now." I wanted to kick her in the caboose, but I tried to keep it soft.

"Oh, yes, we know. His big chance to kill or maim another boy with his hands. Or maybe have it happen to him. Your idea, sir, of what a mother bears and raises her child to do? Your idea of what the good Lord intended his children to devote their lives to undertaking? I don't think so, Mr. Hackett."

The old man came over beside her now to add his two cents.

"Vera's right, Mr. Hackett. We raised Georgie to be a decent boy. Gave him three fine meals a day and the right kind of a home. We've taught him the word of the Lord from the day he was old enough to listen. Kind of hoped he'd go on to spread it in his own way in time. It's what we were aiming for. You can see how she'd feel having him end this way. It's not right. You know it, sir."

I didn't know what was right, never have for anybody else. For myself, if it comes easy, without thinking it out, it's right. I guess it's different for others. All I knew was that Georgie was a lot better off now than he figured to be the night I took him out of one of the sleaziest fight clubs I hope never to be in again.

I'd seen him by accident, and he looked like a good thing. I offered to take him on, bring him east, make a real honest-to-God fighter out of him. He said he couldn't on account of his folks, but I talked him out of that easy enough. He gave them some line about carrying on their work in the east, and he left town with me.

The only time I made a move was when they tried to walk Georgie out of the room. His eyes were misty, empty. He was holding, stupid-like, to everything the woman was saying. He was murmuring, "Yeah, Ma. Sure, Ma. Of course I do. You know I do—" and stuff like that. Putting myself in front of the door, I took Georgie by one arm. I never saw anything like it! Here was this alert, quick-thinking kid who'd never really seen trouble in the ring yet, wearing the sort of look you see on guys who are already walking on their heels.

"Georgie, we got business Friday. You know what it means. We cop this one, we start writing our own ticket. You don't need to listen to this crap. Take it from me, it's bad for these people to be around you. They don't understand what we're after. You've got to get them out of here, Georgie, you hear me?

He didn't say a thing. Seemed as if he couldn't hear me and hardly knew where he was.

"All right, everybody, get the hell out of here—and fast! Can't you see what you're doing—"

"Bengy." He was still staring straight ahead. "Don't talk to them that way. They're my folks."

They were his folks and he listened to them. I knew I didn't have a prayer. But I kept hoping. I do that. Looking back, I guess I should have let them take him the hell out of town on the next train like they wanted to. But instead I told them that if they tried to get Georgie out of Chi before the fight I'd have him dragged back no matter where they took him, and have him thrown in the hoosegow.

"And furthermore," I told them, "I'll see that they throw the key away." I started talking about my "big" connections in Chi and how I was just the guy who could fix it.

That jail bit got them, I guess. They yammered for a while among themselves, and finally Georgie persuaded them to let him go through with this one last fight—but only this one. Then back to Dakota. The old lady let loose a string of curses at me before she left.

Georgie tried to tell me he was sorry.

"It's all right, son. Just be at the weigh-in Friday at three. Remember what I said. I'm not kidding." I heard myself talking loud—not yelling—down the hall at the five of them. My voice sounded funny to me.

I never spoke to Georgie Knize again. I saw him that Friday at the weigh-in. I was on one side of the room with a sportswriter friend. Georgie was on the other side with his family. The sportswriter was the only one in town who hadn't really rapped the fight. He didn't say it had the makings of another Dempsey-Firpo

41

go, but he did lay off. That was enough for me. If the others had just laid off—who knows, maybe it wouldn't have made a difference anyhow. Georgie left his mother's side once—to get up on the scales when the boxing commissioner called his name. As he stood there with just a towel on, he looked small and weak next to Rinaldo. He was a different kid from the one I had known. Even Tom, my sportswriter friend, could see it, and he asked me about it. He wanted to know if Georgie was sick or something. I laughed that one off.

Practically always, I'm with my fighter right up to ring time. That night was different. When I got to the door of Georgie's dressing room, his old man was standing there.

"What do you want here?" he asked me.

All of a sudden I didn't know. "You're planning to second him tonight? You planning to tell your boy how to keep from getting his head punched off?"

"Don't worry, sir. We read in the paper where Georgie does very well at fighting." They sure as hell hadn't read it in a Chicago paper. "He'll do all right without you tonight. Then we take him back home on the train tomorrow."

"Did Georgie say he didn't want me in the ring with him tonight?"

"Yes. Yes. That's what he said. We—none of us—want any more to do with you, Mr. Hackett. We're going home away from big fights and blood money."

Just then I saw the old lady and the kids coming down the corridor. I said the hell with it. If anything good was going to happen in that ring, it'd have to happen without me. I shrugged and walked out towards the stadium. I found Tom in the press section and he made room for me.

"What the hell's going on, Bengy?"

"Don't know, kid. Feel sort of groggy. Been feeling bad all week. Afraid I can't even make it up the steps. Georgie's going to have to do it alone tonight."

Everything after that was foggy. I heard the roar when Rinaldo came in. Not much for Georgie, a few boos but nothing real vicious. Nothing like the yell of murder they were to give out with almost thirty years later when I had Johnny London on his way. It seemed like every drop of blood had been drained out of Georgie as he stood up there in the middle of the ring with Rinaldo, getting the word from the ref. I don't remember seeing the old lady or the other kids around. The father was in Georgie's corner with a kid I knew who was quick at fixing up bad ones around the eyes.

I don't remember any of the fight very clearly. All I knew was Georgie was getting hell beat out of him. Somewhere around the fifth. I started to push my way up to his corner between rounds. The father started cursing me and when Georgie saw me he looked right through me. He didn't want me any more than the rest of them did then. I gave up.

About six minutes later Georgie Knize was dead. He only fell once. He was wide open for the one that finished it. When I saw him drop and lie there without moving, I knew it was bad. Georgie was in good shape. I knew Rinaldo didn't have a punch to put him out like that—even hitting him wide open like he did. He must have landed wrong—or something else, I thought. The word that he was dead got down to the press before it got to the crowd.

"Bengy, get the hell out of here. Go to my hotel and lock yourself in. It's going to be bad."

Tom shoved the key in my hand. I started out the aisle, and another writer whose name I never knew stood up and blocked me. He put his face right up next to mine and said, "We're gonna get you for this, you son of a bitch. Every paper in town will tell what a stinking, lousy—"

I hit him hard. Didn't get too much behind it because there was pushing and moving all around us. He went down, though, and I saw some blood on a couple of chairs. I kept pushing out to the aisle and got out of the place as fast as I could. For a moment I saw the old dame's face come out of the crowd. She was holding something sharp and jagged in her hand. Whatever it was came my way and hit a young kid behind me when I ducked. I kept moving. I got a taxi outside and gave the driver Tom's hotel address.

"How'd it go in there?" The cabbie jabbed his thumb toward the stadium.

"Rinaldo won."

"Yeah, that's what everybody said. The boys were giving ten to one on him. Easy, wasn't it?"

"Yeah," I said. "Pretty easy."

I'd had a couple of drinks by the time Tom got to the hotel. Tom had had a couple, too. Real fast I gave it to him—the whole business about the mother and the rest of the family. Tom listened and he believed me. But it wasn't any use.

"Ben, I had to write it the way I did. They would have killed the story and rewritten it if I'd tried another angle. Besides, they

all got the old lady's word for it. They were doing it up good when I left the stadium. She says Georgie was sick and pleaded with you not to make him fight. She says they all begged you but you told them to go to hell. Told 'em you had too much dough on Georgie's just being in there—no matter in what shape."
I'd felt pretty sick up to then. Now I was scared.
In a little while there was a knock on the door. It was a bellhop with all the morning papers Tom had ordered. Pictures of Georgie, alive and dead, were on every front page. Pictures of the mother, weeping, looking at Georgie. And pictures of me—happy and laughing! Pictures taken a long time before. There was one taken five, six years before. They made 'em out to be me that night. They had me saying, "Accidents will happen." Quoted me half a dozen other ways—all bad. They all knew it was a mismatch from the start, they said. But I was the only one close enough to it to be able to tell it might be Georgie's last fight. On an inside page one of the promoters gave his story. Said he'd decided a few weeks ago that maybe Georgie didn't belong in the same ring with Rinaldo after all. Said he'd offered me an out—and I'd turned him down. Said I admitted that I felt the same way but needed the dough.

"What do you think, Tom?"

"How much money have you got?"

"Around a hundred bucks."

"You're going to have to get into something else. They'll play this story the same way all around the country. You won't have any room to move with so many guys ready to hit you with it."

"Hell, Tom," I said. "I know it's always bad for the manager when his fighter gets the business up there in front of everybody. The advance notices on this one aren't going to help, either. But it'll blow over. It always does."

He was staring up at the ceiling from the bed with his hands under his head. "Not this time, Ben. They're out to get you. Too many guys around waiting for the opening they got tonight. You're through in boxing—for good."

Barney watched me over the rim of his glass and asked me if I'd have another drink. I said I would. Barney had a pretty good idea, I guess, of what happened to me after that. I drifted around from one thing to another—for a while I was even making big dough in bootlegging—and gradually I edged back into fighting. But it wasn't easy; there were always some guys around to spread the whispers to the guys who didn't already know. Even after twenty-five years there were some guys who wouldn't let it lie.

In the meantime I'd met and married Ruth, and that was fine expect for the times when I 'd quit my job because I'd found what I thought was another Georgie Knize.

Barney and I were having a laugh when Johnny and the girl came back. They were laughing and talking together like they were when they left to case the joint.

You might not be able to tell Johnny now from the kid I met ten months ago. He was wearing a grey suit this night, made from a lot better stuff than the blue one we got that day from Harry, and made for him, not some other guy. He had the best build I'd seen since Baer, and if ever a guy didn't need his stuff made for him it was Johnny. Funny the kind of stuff he picked out for himself— quiet, no flashy colors or nothing. Some of it was almost funeral stuff. Whatever it was, it looked great on him. It would have taken a lot worse tailor than Harry to make it look bad.

They came over, yakking it up big over something and she holding on to his arm like she owned him. The way he was looking down at her, maybe she did already.

"Well, Johnny, how do you like our little place?"

"Just great, Mr. Ellis. I think I'll be coming over here more often." He winked at the girl. She laughed.

"Don't you think you'd better check that with Mr. Hackett, Johnny?"

"Anything that keeps him winning big is O.K. with me, Miss Ellis. We gotta be rolling now. Ruth'll be expecting us and we got a long day tomorrow."

We all walked down to the car together, me talking to Barney and them trailing along behind, kind of quiet. I hopped up in front and started the motor. Johnny just kept talking to the girl 'til I yelled for him to get in.

"See you tomorrow, Johnny!"

"It's definite! 'Night, Mr. Ellis."

We drove for a while, not saying a thing. Johnny switched on the radio and was humming along with the music. It seemed like he was in another county. We were going over the George Washington Bridge when he said, "Ben, how old were you when you and Ruth got married?'

"I was thirty-five. She was twenty-four or five. I forget which. Why?"

"No reason. Just interested."

We didn't talk the rest of the way back or after we got there. He went right in his room and shut the door.

The Patrick fight was a week off and I was worried. Maybe Patrick didn't have a left hook like "Kid" Kaplan. He didn't need to at the rate we were going. Up to then, Johnny was the best fighter in training I'd seen. He did everything right the first time you told him. It was like you just had to remind him how he used to do it right a long time ago somewhere. But it wasn't like that at all now. I'd be telling him something and it was like he was a million miles away. The next minute he was doing the exact wrong thing I told him not to.

That Tuesday it was so bad I was even thinking of calling Doniger in Boston and telling him we'd have to pull out for a week or two anyway. That would go over just great after all the trouble I had getting him to go for the story that I had a boy who, after seven fights, was in Patrick's class. Patrick was plenty popular around the Hub and was in the middle of his own winning streak of nine. Up to now I'd had no doubts at all Johnny was ready for him. Now it looked to me as if he'd have trouble taking the guys he'd already put away.

When Johnny came back to his stool at the end of the third round that day, there was a cut over his right eye, running like a small river! I jumped up in the ring, sore as hell, running over to the other corner.

"What the hell happened?" I yelled at Lenny.

"It was an easy one," Lenny said. "He's blocked a thousand of 'em this week. For no reason he just dropped his guard when I was throwin' it."

I walked back over to Johnny's corner where a guy was working on the eye. It didn't look so bad now with the adrenaline chloride getting to work.

"How's it look? Can he work this afternoon?"

"Sure, sure. It's nothin'. A scratch. He could go back in now, if he'd keep awake."

"We'll play it safe. Three o'clock we'll try again."

"It was my fault, Ben. I don't know why—just dropped my guard," Johnny said. "It won't happen again."

"Glad to hear it. Just do it once against Patrick and we'll be workin' with the ice packs—in the dressing-room."

"I said it won't happen again, for Christ's sake."

He pulled his robe around him and slid out through the ropes.

It was three-forty when Johnny showed up that afternoon with the girl. They came rolling down the driveway in her new white convertible, looking like they didn't have a care in the world. She was driving and he had one arm around her shoulder. When they pulled up where the driveway stops about fifty yards from the ring he didn't even bother to climb right out. Just sat in there talking to her a couple more minutes like there was nothing else in the world to think about.

When they did climb out I found it tough to believe I was seeing right. He was still wearing his boxing shorts but the rest of the way he was made up for tennis! I saw the rackets in the back of her car when they drove up but I didn't figure Johnny would even think of... of all the stupid ways he could pull something by moving fast in the wrong direction. Of course, she was wearing a special-made tennis dress that did everything for a figure that didn't need a thing done for it.

I went down and met them about halfway between the driveway and the ring. I blew up once that day. I was going to try to keep it in hand this time. Johnny was smiling sort of sheep-like.

"Gee, Ben, I'm sorry, no kiddin'. Rain was showing me how to play tennis and the time just went. It's great! It oughta help keep my muscles loose. I'll get my shoes on. Be right out. See you later, Rain."

The way he said it and the look he gave her—Christ!

Rain came up to me. "Ben, I really am sorry. I should have known better."

"Yeah. You should have. You did."

I started away from her, but she came after me, grabbed my arm and turned me around. "Look, I said I was sorry. What do you want me to do?"

I looked in her eyes, trying to get an idea of what she was really thinking. The blue was on fire, all right and it looked like maybe the tears weren't too far behind.

"You want to know—honest?"

She looked at me, hard. The fire was still there but there wasn't going to be any tears.

"No, I don't think I do... I'm sure I don't. I don't think I'll watch the workout, either. Would you tell Johnny I'll see him at the resort whenever he's finished... I'll be in my room."

"Sure, I'll tell him."

She turned around, sharp, and started back for the car.

After the workout, Johnny was in a pretty good mood. As we walked back to the clubhouse, he said, "Looked better than this morning, huh, Ben?"

"Couldn't a looked worse. How'd it feel?"

"One hundred percent better. Look, I know you're sore about

47

it, but I really think that tennis was just what—"

That did it. "Goddammit!" I said. "Let's get something straight right now. Are you gonna follow my orders—all of them, or are you gonna take off on your own? We might as well get it straight right now, because—"

"Sure I am, Ben. I always have. If I thought you'd be sore... "

"All right, kid. That's all I want. Let's not say anything else about it... yeah, one more thing. I don't want you running out like you did this morning before Tony has a chance to give you your rub. Don't you know you could undo a week's work that way?"

"Yeah, you're right. I know it. It won't happen again. I mean it."

It sounded, at the time, like he meant it.

"I'm going in the bar a minute. I'll be right in with you," I said.

"Bring me a double Scotch, will you? Black and White."

"If I ever catch you—"

He punched me easy on the arm, laughing. I rolled with it and it looked like things were going to be O.K. After I got a couple of jolts in me I was sure of it. When I came in the locker room, he'd finished his shower and Tony was rubbing him down. I sank down into one of the big easy chairs Barney just lately put around.

"You hungry, kid?"

"I'll say."

"I know a great steak place we can go to in Tappan—the '76 House."

"Gee, Ben, I'd like to. But couldn't we do it another time? I've kind of got a thing on... well... "

"With the girl?"

"That's right."

"I thought we settled that outside just now."

"I don't think so."

"You didn't tell me you were going to do what I told you—all the time?"

"Ben, you can tell me to go out and run fifty miles before breakfast, to box Lenny eighty rounds with my right tied behind me, to go on a diet of tomato juice and potato pancakes... "

"What the hell are you talking about?"

"Just that you can tell me to do anything that has to do with boxing or training and I'll do it, even if it seems crazy—because I know it'll be right, I'll be better for it in the long run. But when you tell me I can't like or go out with a swell kid like Rain, then... "

"Johnny, why do you think they keep wives out of training camps? Not just sweethearts, but wives—even the old fat ones?"

"She's not my wife and she's... not my sweetheart. I don't figure to ever get that lucky. She's just a nice girl I like who's been pretty swell to me and I don't see anything wrong with—"

"Nice girl!" He almost knocked Tony over, coming up quick from lying on the table.

"I told you I didn't want to hear any of that! If you've got anything to say about her say it to her face, but don't tell me! It doesn't make any difference—whatever it is."

"O.K., kid. I'll see you tonight or in the morning. We're going to stay out here for the last two nights before we knock off training. I got a date with a steak. So long." I figured I'd be lucky to get a little soup down. Those things always get me in the gut.

I guess I must have drove a couple of hours, trying to get it straight on what I ought to do. I would've liked to talk to Ruth and almost called her once or twice. She was staying with Joe and Margaret for the week and I didn't want them to hear what was going on—even get an idea I was worried. I was sure Ruth would be able to tell and might likely say something about it in front of them. I decided not to call.

I stopped off at one of those neon hamburger joints on Route 9 and was just about able to make it with half a burger and coffee.

When I got back I knew I was still too edgy to get any shuteye. I could tell by the noise and lights in the clubhouse that the boys were living it up. I didn't much want to sit in a hand or get in the middle of anything. I decided to go for a walk and took a path that ran up in the woods and came out on a part of the lake where nobody ever went. It was hot and I figured on maybe going for a swim. Walking along and thinking about the heat, I wondered if maybe it could be what was bothering Johnny. It never seemed to before. His weight was O.K. I'd check on whether he was taking the salt tablets like I told him to. It was a lucky thing he could take them. I know some guys puke every time they try to get one down. For keeping your strength up in the dog-days, you can't beat them.

I could just about feel myself uncoiling as I walked along. After going a few yards down the path I couldn't hear any of the noise from the clubhouse, nothing but crickets, or once in a while a little animal or bird. This was the life after a good working day. I took off my clothes, piled them a ways off the path, and started paddling. The water was warm and soft. I swam out to a small island about fifty yards away and pulled myself up on the shore and let myself down easy on the grass. I was breathing kind of

49

hard. I thought of the way Ruth always kids me about not being in shape when I do a little job around the house and end up kind of sweaty and tired, but always with a big glass of iced tea or something ready for me—"Here," she'd say, "I was just going to have this but you look like you need it more than I do." All of a sudden I missed her like hell and wished I had her with me right then. If it wasn't too late when I got back I was going to call her. I didn't figure on sounding worried now. If I did, it was just too bad.

I lay there for about ten minutes with my hands under my head, looking up at the moon and stars. I lifted myself upon one elbow and was just going to let myself slide back into the water when the headlights of a car came running out over the lake. There is a road big enough for a car to travel running down to the lake from the main camp drive that stops a couple of hundred yards away. The car pulled up about twenty feet from where I stowed my gear. The lights snapped out and I saw it was the white convertible. The moon was a spotlight on them and made it so's I could see them as clear as if it was day. Rain was wearing one of them blue dancing-type gowns with no shoulders and Johnny was wearing one of those country club white jackets I didn't even know he had.

They didn't waste any time talking. When the lights went out they both just moved together as if a magnet or something was in charge. He was kissing her all over her face and hair and shoulders and she was running her hand through his hair and over his back. Then she leaned back, pushing him away. With a quick move of her arm and flip of her wrist, she undid his black bow tie and jumped out her side of the car. She started running back up the path. He sat there a sec, surprised, and then jumped out and started after her, just at a jog but moving about three times as fast as she was. They went around a corner of the path and out of sight. It was the stillest night ever and I could hear them laughing and shouting. Then it all stopped for a couple of minutes. There wasn't a sound. I just lay there, hoping they'd decide to go home or even back to the dance, or whatever, so's I could come on in and get my clothes.

When I saw them again he was carrying her, she with her arms around his neck and kissing his chest. Neither of them seemed to be wearing anything. He put her down gentle on the grass and, honest to Christ, I knew it wasn't right, but—I watched.

It was a good half hour later when they got back into the car and drove off. I almost couldn't hear the motor anymore when I got up and dropped back into the water. I swam in quick with none of the good relaxed feeling I had on the way out. I climbed out and went over to my clothes. I dressed in a hurry and started back.

The games had broken up and all the guys sacked in by the time I made it to the clubhouse. I was glad I didn't need to see anybody on the way upstairs. When I got up in the room Johnny and I shared he wasn't there, so I figured they must've headed back to the resort for a while. There was a note on the table saying Ruth called while I was out, and asking me to call her in the morning.

I was in bed, but not asleep when Johnny came in about ten minutes later. He was humming something to himself, soft. He bumped into a table.

"Put on the small light if you want. I'm not asleep."
"Gee, I thought you would be. It's kind of late."
"Yeah, I know. Have a good time?"
"Yeah."

I decided on letting it go 'til morning. If we got on it now we'd most likely wake the whole goddam house. But it was going to have to come up.

I didn't sleep more than two hours that night—if I got that much. The alarm went off at seven. I pulled myself out, yawning and stretching. Johnny just lay there snoozing like nothing was happening with the clock hollering in his ear. It ran itself out and he still didn't move. Usually he was downstairs having his tea before I was even finished dressing. I went over to the bed and shook him, not too gentle. He mumbled something and turned over on his other side, pulling the blanket up over his head.

"Goddammit, get up! We got work to do!"
"Yeah, yeah. Just a minute or two more, Ben. I'm tired."
"Well, what the hell did you expect after running around all night?"
"Um?"

I figured he didn't hear me. "Just get your tail out of there and let's get going."

"Sure, Ben. Just one more minute."

I went to the table and got the pitcher. I filled it in the bathroom, ice cold, and came back over to the bed. I gave him the whole thing, right on the head. He came up, ready for action.

"Goddammit! What's the idea? I said I was getting up."

"Yeah, I know. Of course, Patrick has most likely done five miles and a couple of rounds up in New England somewhere by now. But that's O.K. We'll catch up with him, won't we?"

51

Johnny laughed and started to pull on his sweat clothes.

"You're really worried about this one, aren't you? What's the story? You haven't gone and over-matched me, have you?"

"Look, if you—"

"Take it easy. I was just kidding. I'll take out Patrick in four. Any bets?"

"It sounds good. That's about what I figured when we started getting ready for this one. You haven't been oozing much confidence the last coupla days."

"Aw, I'm O.K. You know, yesterday—that was nothing. I just got careless and… "

"Yeah, O.K., kid. But I think you'll just do your roadwork and exercises today and tomorrow. Maybe some work on the bags. I got an idea maybe we been doing a little too much sparring this trip."

"Yeah."

He finished lacing up his sneaker and stood up. He stood there a minute like he was thinking deep about something.

I had a bad feeling that I wasn't going to like whatever it was. I almost wished he'd let it go for the time.

"I'm going to marry Rain, Ben. Right after the fight. I didn't think anything close to this could ever happen to me… but, she said 'yes'… well, almost. I think it's going to take, no kidding."

I felt dizzy and sat down on the bed. He thought I was doing it as something funny and laughed.

"Now, take it easy, Dad. It's not really that… "

"Don't call me Dad!"

I snapped it out, angry, in almost a kind of yell. I don't know what the hell got into me. Maybe he came too close to what I was feeling for a long time. Maybe he'd become a lot more than a fighter—the fighter—to me. Whatever it was, I was ashamed of it. He didn't say a thing, just looked at me real funny. I glared back at him.

I went downstairs and out. I walked down the path to the ring and planted myself in one of the chairs sitting around. Then I saw the blue notebook lying on the chair next to me. There was a gum sticker on the lower part of it with the name of the owner—Rain Ellis. I picked it up and opened it. It was full of notes. Like about boxing being something around 2,600 years old, about whether it was first (1) a discipline, (2) an exercise, or (3) an art; Homer's views on fights as part of public ceremonies; a guy named Horace rating boxers ahead of poets; the way the cestus went from something made from pieces of rawhide to something made from pieces of lead, brass, and iron; and there being lots of proof of

"British hardihood" giving us boxing like we got it today. For my dough, Tommy Farr was pretty good, but after that, well... Then was a whole lot of stuff under "Social Strata of the Boxer Today." There was a bunch of boxes and lines under that one. The whole thing went to show she was picking up a lot of real dope about fighting—like hell!

"Trying to improve yourself, Mr. Hackett?"

I almost jumped out of my skin. She was standing right behind me. She was wearing blue jeans and a khaki shirt and looking about sixteen years old—until you looked where it was easiest to tell. I handed her the book.

"Oh, no, I can wait," she said, "if you think it'll help you adjust yourself to society."

She was talking different now than she did before. In a way, she was trying to win me over before—but not now. She was saying now she didn't care, she'd got what she wanted—Johnny. I could go to hell.

"You think I need—adjusting?"

"You need a lot more than that, I think. I don't know what, but... I tried my best to—"

"To ruin the best damn piece of fighter I ever had going. Maybe you've made the grade, lady, I don't know."

She twisted her face up in a frown—it looked good even that way—as if she couldn't at all figure what I was talking about. When she turned away from me a minute and was looking out over the lake I couldn't help but think of the way I saw her last night. She turned back to me. This time there was no doubt about her eyes being wet. She was biting her lip for a minute and then she said,

"Do you really want me to be honest with you?"

"Do you think you know how any more?"

"I don't get it, Ben Hackett. I just don't get it—this thing you've got against me. Maybe it's just a feeling, I don't know..."

"It's no feeling."

"All right, it's no feeling. It's real. It doesn't make any difference, not any more. You say I'm ruining Johnny. It's not so. You don't—I don't ruin someone I love. And, well, there you are."

"Sure, here I am... with a prelim boy who could have been champ—great."

"Are you serious?"

"Honey, I'm so far past being serious it ain't funny."

"Well, then, how can you say that? You think Johnny's a great fighter. How can my being in—"

"He's a hell of a long way from being a great fighter. He's good, got all the stuff to get there—I think. But, he won't—ever—at this rate."

"And it's my fault if he doesn't?"

"That's right. Maybe it ain't easy to understand, I don't know. You don't just become champ, it's not something you fall into. Maybe you fall into it if you got the right ones behind you—Johnny ain't. All he's got is me and his own two hands. It would've been enough—until you come along."

She shook her head, like she wasn't even close. "But that's not the whole story, is it, Mr. Hackett? There are other reasons you don't want Johnny to love me, aren't there?"

"Isn't that one enough?"

"Not when you're in love."

"Would it be too tough to take a rain-check on it?" I said. "Couldn't you hop a train to—"

"Yes, it would be… too tough. I'm sorry."

"You don't care if he makes it, then?"

She thought about that one a while, too.

"Maybe I don't."

"That's sweet, too. He'd be glad to hear it."

"I've told him."

"You what?"

"I told him I wasn't sure I wanted him to become a champion. I've known some and seen some."

A taxi pulled up in front of the clubhouse. A woman got out and came down toward us. A few more steps and I saw it was Ruth! I couldn't believe it for a minute, but I couldn't be wrong once she got close. She was moving different, somehow—quicker, lighter, more like she used to when we first met. She was wearing a light, frilly blue dress and a little white hat I never saw before. It was like she was taking big gulps of the air, coming down the path. She looked about ten years younger than I was used to thinking of her. Slimmer, too, it seemed. Until she got up right close to us she could have almost been the young model I first met over at Joe's when he brought me home for dinner after work that night.

I got up and came to meet her when I saw who it was. I must've hugged her a little rougher than I meant to. It felt good.

"Ben, Ben. Take it easy, boy… oh, there goes my hat. I spent twenty minutes getting it to sit right this morning. Thanks very much!"

"I'm sorry, hon. Gosh, it's just so great to see you. You look wonderful. What you been doing to yourself?"

She got a little red at that.

"Shh. Really, Ben. I just bought this hat and dress yesterday. That must make the difference."

"Naw, naw. It's a lot more than that. But why'd ya decide to come over? Weren't Joe and Margaret treatin' my girl right?"

"Yes, yes. They were fine. I just missed you so much. And then, last night, when you didn't call or anything I started to worry. I know it was stupid, but I did. I woke up early this morning, and the worried feeling was still there. I decided to just go and get the first bus. Is everything really all right—with both of you?"

"Yeah, pretty much all right."

"Pretty much?"

"That's about all. Johnny just doesn't seem so sharp as usual for this one. I'm not gonna have him spar anymore before the fight. Maybe he's overworked. That's what Barney thought. Me, I doubt that's the real—"

"Good heavens, is it possible Ben Hackett doesn't really hate every woman on earth? In other words, it's just me, me personally. I had so hoped it was just a matter of my unfortunate sex. How do you do? I'm Rain Ellis."

I didn't see her get up and come over to us.

"Ruth Hackett. Ben has told me about you."

There was a gap. They stood looking at each other, hard. The girl fidgeted in a jean pocket for some cigarettes. She took one out and lit it, and I saw her hand was shaking a little.

"He has, huh? Then I guess you hate my guts, too?" Rain said.

"Why, no."

"You don't? That's strange, to say the least."

"Why?"

"Well, don't you think I'm going to ruin his fighter? Wouldn't that mean you couldn't get all the new hats and dresses you like, and all the things after that?"

"Are you going to ruin Johnny?"

She came out with a fake kind of half-laugh at that. She stopped it quick, in a kind of cough.

"Believe me, Mrs. Hackett, there's nobody in this whole stupid world I'd like less to hurt than Johnny."

"I guess maybe Ben thinks you'll hurt him without wanting to," Ruth said. "Is it possible?"

"I honestly don't know. I know I have to be with him. If that's going to hurt him, well… "

"Yes, if that's going to hurt him, then?"
"It won't. It can't! That's all. In the long run, it'll have to be—"
I took Ruth by the arm. "C'mon, honey. This isn't goin' anywhere. Why get in the middle of somethin' you don't have to?"
"But I do have to, Ben. This affects me as much as it does you—now, this time. As Miss Ellis pointed out, perhaps this means the difference between how many new hats and dresses I'll be able to get next month."
The girl broke in, "I didn't mean—"
"I know you didn't. Don't worry about it. Everything will work itself out all right, I think."
"If you can convince your husband of that, you've got yourself a friend for life—if you want one."
"I'd like it."
Now, glad as I was before to see Ruth, I was wishing she had stayed home. The thing was going to be enough trouble without having her against me too. The way things were drifting, it looked like the odds on it were pretty good. The girl was looking at her with this big grateful look, made you feel funny inside. It wasn't tough to tell Ruth liked her, too.
"Honey, let me drive you back to the resort. You don't want to hang around here. There's plenty to do up there, and we'll be around to pick you up early in the afternoon."
"I do want to see Johnny first. You know, I was worried about him, too. I'd like to see, with my own eyes, that he's all right."
I shrugged and went over to a chair by the ring to make some notes. Leastways, that's what I made out to be doing. I just didn't want to stand there, watching the thing get out of hand. If it was going to, it wasn't likely there was much I could do about it. My being there would most likely just make it come off more so. They went on chatting, only not so serious. Soon they were even having a couple of small laughs together. Nothing could've made me laugh right then. It was funny how the two of them seemed to mesh right away, like there was some big common thing between them. I didn't, for the life of me, see what the hell it could be.
They were really hitting it off when Johnny came jogging out of the woods at the end of his first trip around the lake. He came running over.
"Hey, Ruth, what are you doing here? Gee, you look like something out of one of those fashion magazines. New duds?"
"You know, soon I'll be believing this, if I hear any more of it. Yes, Johnny, new duds. Thank you for them."
"Are you kidding?"

"Not at all. I told you once you were going to be driving a great big gravy train. It looks like you're already at the throttle."

Johnny laughed. "Rain, will you listen to that? When I first came to the Hacketts' I didn't have much more than a nickel to my name, I was sleeping in the park, and my clothes were falling off my back, no kidding. So what do they do? They take me in and feed me and dress me and give me a roof over my head. No matter how many fights I win I could never—"

"You were an investment, Johnny. Now you're starting to pay off."

"O.K., Ruth, whatever you say. According to some people, your stock isn't too high right now."

"How do you feel about it?" Ruth asked.

"Why don't you come up to Boston with us? I'll show you then what I think. Patrick, too." Johnny grinned at her.

"I came up this morning, because I was worried about you, Johnny. No more."

"Good."

It didn't seem to me the chow-chow was getting anywhere. Dames shouldn't be let in training camps any time.

"You're gonna get cold standin' around. How many times do I have to tell you? Do two more laps around and then knock off. Get goin'!"

"See you later, gang!" He didn't even deal me in on that one. Just included the two of them. He jogged away, back toward the woods, looking back over his shoulder and waving just before he went in.

"It's really been a pleasure, Mrs. Hackett. I wouldn't have thought it possible, but it has. Please see if you can't ... well, you know."

"Yes, I know. I'll see what we can do."

She reached out, quick, grabbed Ruth's hand, like she'd just promised her a million bucks, and started up towards the club-house. We watched her move off with that walk that had to do something to any guy whether he liked it or not. I turned around to Ruth.

"Thanks a lot, kid!"

"For what, Ben?"

"For nothin'! For lining up on the other side of the fence, across from me, that's what! Don't you think maybe I've got enough trouble with those two without having you go over in the other camp?"

"Ben, come over here—please."

57

When she talked like that there wasn't a damn thing I could do except what she wanted. We went over and sat down in a couple of chairs by the ring. She took my hand in hers and held it.

"Are you absolutely sure—please try to understand me, I don't know—there have to be two sides? They seem like such a swell couple of kids, and—"

"Seem is right. Wrapped you right around her little finger, didn't she? She always could talk pretty; that came natural. Could do it just around the time she could walk. I can see how it would get you, believe me. Just before you came up I was listening to her for a couple of minutes there the way I used to when she was a kid. She can still talk pretty, I won't argue that. Only this is how she knows how to put it to use, like she didn't used to. You hang around the kind of people she's been hanging around long enough and you learn all the angles. It don't take long. She learns fast."

"It just didn't seem the way—not for a minute. I don't really think I'm so bad at sizing people up and—"

"Well, you're wrong this time, Ruth. I don't see why you even try to argue with me about it. You just met her and talked to her for a couple minutes, and right away you know her inside out."

"It's such an important thing, Ben, you can't take a chance on being wrong. I don't think I've seen two kids more in love. If we ever did anything that damaged what they have and then found out we were wrong... "

"Just a minute, Ruth. Look, when you say 'we' most of the time, it makes me proud as hell, and makes me feel as good as I ever could inside. But this time, it ain't a thing we're gonna do or decide about. You can't be expected to know much of the story, or try to figure the way it's got to end up, if somebody don't step in."

"Don't get me angry, Ben. It's a fairly simple problem. I think maybe you're adding a lot to it that isn't really there."

"Yeah, come to think of it, it is pretty simple. I guess maybe you can understand this. Do you think it's good for them to be rolling around in the grass a couple of days before a fight he knows will be his toughest? You know we're at the point where, if we get slowed up or stopped, we can go shooting back so fast it'll take your breath away."

"How do you know?"

"Because this boy Patrick is supposed to have a couple of—"

"No. I mean about their... sleeping together."

"I saw them."

"You... you... " She was looking at me like she couldn't believe me. "What can you mean? Did you... "

"No, I haven't been peeping in keyholes and looking for it. I went for a swim last night. Went out to a little island through the forest over there. I was lying out there, resting, and minding my own business, when they came driving up in her convertible, and parked over where I'd come from, just about where I stowed my clothes. The moon was out, and I really had me a ringside seat."

"You mean you watched... all of it?"

"I thought I just said."

I was making it sound as bad as I could, almost like now I was glad I did it and didn't feel a thing bad about it. I was that sore at her for the way she took up with the girl, knowing how I felt about her.

"You're nothing but a damn... You've had some—crazy—feelings about sex, but I never thought... "

"Don't start that, Ruth. I don't know where you get some of the things you do. Maybe I been letting you stay home a little bit too much by yourself. Too much reading, you know, ain't good. You get too far ahead of me. Then we can't talk together right any more."

"We haven't really been talking together, or doing anything else together for years, Ben. I think now I'm beginning to see why. I thought for a long while it was just the money and the way you felt about fighting, and everything. I'm beginning to realize that hasn't been the trouble at all, maybe a little of it, but not much. If we really felt what we should about each other, I guess those things wouldn't have made too much difference. At least we would have been able to work them out better than we did."

"It seems a funny time to start talking like this, kid."

"It's not the kind of thing you pick a time for, I'm afraid, Ben. Why is it a funny time now?"

"Well, just when it looks like maybe we got everything breaking right for us. Like maybe now I'm goin' to be able to give you all the things I've wanted to right along, the things you should of had since you was born. It can be a hell of a good life from here on in. No kiddin', it can."

"You really think so?"

I put my arm around her and tried to give my answer everything. If it came across the way I felt it, that would be enough. "I know it."

She patted me on the arm. I wasn't sure what it meant. I was afraid maybe it was a kind of "there, there," like you might give to a kid who was hurt. I hoped that wasn't it.

"What about it?"

"About it?"

"Are you... gonna be in my corner... all the way?"

I don't know what happened to me then. But I seemed to crack inside, or something. I started shaking—and crying. It was the first time since I was a kid and it didn't happen much then. I pushed my face down into my hands. Ruth put her hand on the back of my neck and stroked it easy, the way she used to do. It was a long time ago. She knew it was no act.

"Don't worry, Ben. It'll work out. You're tired. You'll make it—with or without me."

"I won't, Ruth. Believe me. I won't. I need you to make it."

I pulled at my eyes and straightened up. It wasn't my idea of the way to go.

"If that's the case," she said, "you'll probably find me around."

We sat there awhile, close together, looking at the empty ring.

Three

"I'm blind, Your Grace. Only let me see my man and he shall not beat me yet."

—Jack Broughton

THE OPERATOR said, "There's a Mr. Martell downstairs to see you, Mr. Hackett."

I figured I didn't know how good life was up until then. It was no use stalling with Gino. He never forgot a thing or let it go.

"Tell him to come on up."

I looked out the window at the mist. Never once been in Boston when the weather was anything near what you'd want. I thought maybe this was where all my problems ended—not the way I wanted them to. The knock came at the door. To see Gino alone was a surprise. He didn't come that way often.

"Bengy-boy, y'look like Christmas! How d'ya do it? Yeah, don't tell me. I know, it just takes one good boy, is that it?"

"Could be."

He pulled his coat off and threw it down on a chair. "Could be, hell! I saw him against Murphy and Burns. I got a wad ridin' on him to take out this creep inside of eight. Patrick ain't got nothin', take my word for it. Got lucky with a left a couple of nights in with some bums. Don't mean a thing. This kid o' yours can take a stiff one. You know it. Hey, ya ain't gone done anything so I shouldn'ta put my dough on him, have ya? The kid's too good to fool with now like that."

"No. I ain't done anything. He just ain't been lookin' as good for this one, that's all."

No matter how many times Gino pulls a fast one on you, its' a good idea to play along with him until you can't do it no more. Then's the time you got to start making up your mind as to how much you like living, how much dough it's worth to you and him, and things on those lines.

"I'll make ya a deal."

It was coming now.

"I don't want it, Gino. Johnny's cut up as much as he's going to be. Why don't we talk about something else, since that's how it is?"

Gino pulled out one of those big cigars and lit up, leaning back in the chair. The grin came on.

"I don't want a piece of your boy, Bengy… "

"Then everything's O.K. Just shows how I can go jumping at things, before I—"

"I want all of him. Ain't that romantic?"

We must have sat there about two minutes, not saying a thing. Around that time, he flicked his cigar ashes and leaned forward.

"How much, Bengy? Got some old Hub friends waitin' for me in the bar. Oughta get back to 'em, so let's clean it up, anyhow get it set straight so we can sign the papers tomorrow or the next day. Name it, boy. How much? Don't spare me. I been lucky lately."

"Maybe you ought to watch him tonight before you—"

I don't know what I was hoping to get with the stall.

"I seen all I need to see. He's got it. I've pushed guys up there in the last coupla years didn't have a little bit of what he's got. I'll have him all the way up before next year's over."

"No, you won't, Gino. I'm not selling. Not this time. Maybe it'll be my last crack at the big dough, but I'm having it."

He laughed again. Not so hard this time.

"I guess ya didn't hear me, Bengy. Sometimes I don't talk so clear. I was talkin' big dough before. Ya know I ain't tryin' to highjack your paper with the kid. I just want it—right away. I want to pay for it. Get it now?"

"I got it before."

"Didja? It didn't sound much like it. Just gimme the price, then. I got places to go."

"You better go to 'em, then," I said.

"Ain't it funny? I thought a couple old pals like you and me was gonna be able to work this out in around nothin' flat. Here we are, no further along than when I walked in the door."

"On this deal, Gino, we won't get any further. I been thinkin' the whole thing out ahead of time. I'm takin' Johnny in myself. Maybe you wouldn't see it, but I got a little more than dough ridin' on him."

That really broke him up. "A little more than dough, huh! That's great, Bengy, just great! The boys'll be glad to hear you ain't lost your sense o' humor, anyhow. No matter how the breaks go, you can always count on Bengy for a good one, huh?"

"No joke, Gino."

"No joke? That's too bad, then. Y'know, if it's seein' your name up there again, well, I wouldn'ta minded keepin' ya on— your name, me pullin' the strings, and like that, but on account of Chi I'd feel we wasn't doin' right. London's too good a piece to take that kind of chance with."

"What kind of a chance?'

"We're likely to be on our way, for real, when some jerk writer drags the whole thing up again. It was some story, the way they played it. It wouldn't be the kinda publicity we'd want for Johnny, would it?"

"I don't get it, Gino. What's your point? Nobody's brought it up, so far. Why would—"

"Why? 'Cause Johnny ain't even on his way yet. If somebody dragged it up now, who the hell would know who they was talkin' about? Just a coupla the boys, that's all. It wouldn't mean a thing to them, 'cause they all know it. When he's set for a title-shot, maybe even after he's made it, it'd make a lot better story, don't ya think?"

"I guess if they dragged out your record it'd be good for him? Wasn't there something about a shooting out in Trenton, and a... "

His fists doubled up. For a sec I wished like hell he'd swing on me. There wasn't a chance in the world. He's never been in a fight in his life. If he was he'd lose it. They don't come flabbier or softer than Gino. He got up and walked over to the window, looking out.

"Y'know nobody's gonna drag out nothin' about Gino Martell, don't ya, Bengy? Y'really know that, don't ya?"

I knew it.

"Can't we work somethin' out, now? I'd like to know everythin' was all set when I'm watchin' tonight. Make me feel a lot better."

"I'm sorry, Gino, I—"

The door opened and in came Johnny.

"Took a walk around town, it's a funny kind of... excuse me, I didn't know you... "

"It's O.K., kid. C'mon in. I been wantin' t'meet ya."

"Oh yeah?"

"That's right. 'Fact, Bengy and me was just talkin' about ya. We was wonderin' if everythin' was all set for ya ta get ahead as fast as we know ya oughta."

"I thought I was coming along O.K.," Johnny said.

"Ya are, kid, ya are. But, when ya get up nearer the big dough, the goin' ain't always as easy. Too many guys up there tryin' a keep their meal tickets from gettin' pushed in with a good boy. Sometimes they need a little pushin'. Y'know how it is. We all need it once in a while. We was wonderin' if Bengy's in the best spot to do the pushin' right now."

"Who was wondering, you or Ben? What the hell is this, anyhow? I don't like the sound of it."

"Take it easy, Johnny. We're just tryin' to work out things for your own good. We seen too many boys left just sittin' around lately, waitin' for a crack at somethin' big, until they turned rotten up there on the shelf. We wanna be sure it don't happen to you, that's all."

"Why?"

Gino isn't talked to in that tone of voice much. I was worried. It looked like Johnny didn't know who the hell he was with, or else didn't give a damn. When I was talking to him before, there wasn't much else I could say, because there was just one answer to what he was asking. Still, I tried not to spit it out, the way Johnny was talking now.

"'Cause you're a talent, kid, that's why. When y'love boxin', like we do, it makes you feel lousy to see a talent sittin' around waitin'. Ain't that right, Bengy?"

"I think we'll keep movin'."

"Whadda you think, Johnny? Think you got all the push you're gonna need behind ya right now?"

"Yeah, I think we're O.K. Whatever Ben says is O.K. with me."

"That bein' the case, I guess we can let it hang for a while. We'll see what happens. Either way, stop over to my place sometime when y'get back in town. We'll have a drink, and some fun—any style, you name it. I gotta run. Nice to meet ya, Johnny. We'll be doin' business, sooner or later. Remember, Bengy, y'can pretty much name your price now. It might be different later."

"I'll let you know, Gino, if I change my mind. Don't count on it."

"Funny thing, Bengy—I am countin' on it. See ya."

He went out.

"What did he want?" Johnny wanted to know.

"He wanted to buy your contract—right now. You heard him, said I can pretty much name my own price."

"Try not to have him around any more, Ben, will you? At least not when I might be here. I don't like him. If he can help us, or something, and you have to talk to him, good. But I don't want to see him."

There are plenty of people don't like Gino right off. It's not hard to see. In fact, for me, it's tough to see how anybody ever could like him. Thinking on it now, I bet there ain't one who does. I never saw anybody felt things so quick as Johnny. It was like that with the girl, only in the other direction.

"You got the right slant on him, kid. How'd you get it that quick?"

"I have no slant on him. I just don't like him. I never saw him or heard of him before in my life. What did you say his name is?"

"Gino Martell. He's a big man in boxing now. There's no doubt some of the stuff he said has a lot to it. He could make things fall in line a lot quicker when you reach the 'almost' spot. When he talks, they listen. I think we can make it O.K., without any of that kind of a hand. I ain't sure, so if you—"

"Don't talk crazy, Ben. I'm having nothing to do with that guy, no matter how much weight he pulls. If I was around him long, I know goddam well I'd belt him sooner or later."

"It might be the last time you belted anybody."

"Yeah, well..."

He shrugged his shoulders. Pulling off his shirt, he went into the other room and flopped down on the bed.

"I'm gonna snooze for awhile. Wake me for the fight."

"Sure, kid. Sweet dreams."

Johnny never looked more like a old pro. I got the feeling the two of them was on strings—with Johnny doing all the pulling.

Patrick was a kid with a lot of promise. I could tell that right away. He was about three years older than Johnny, but Johnny was making him look like he was still about one step out of the Golden Gloves. Johnny was in charge all the way, and going into the ninth I figured there was maybe two rounds they could call even. The rest was all Johnny. He was working this night something like Billy Graham. Nothing was wasted. Patrick hit him solid maybe twice, and Johnny came right back. Both times it was rights that landed. It goes to show what a good job Lenny did in getting him ready for the hook. Every time Patrick threw it, which wasn't much at the start, but was plenty now, Johnny would slip and counter neat, or block it with his arm or be rolling with it all the way. It was pretty as hell to watch. Johnny didn't yet have Patrick wobbling at any time, but he had him cut up so bad I figured there was a good chance the ref might stop it. Patrick was a lot better with defense than I figured he was. I saw him once or twice in the gym a couple years back and he'd learned a lot since then. A decision here would be plenty good enough for us. We'd be right on schedule.

The doc came up in Patrick's corner at the end of the eighth and was looking at the cuts above both his eyes. He said something to the ref and I thought maybe they was going to stop it right there. Ever since the Carter-Collins go up there, they been plenty careful they don't get too much blood around. Especially on TV nights, of which this was one. The extra dough it was going to mean was swell, but, more than that, it might be just the break we needed, promotion-wise. Gino couldn't've fixed it better. The doc was getting down out of the ring and it looked like he was saying it was O.K. for things to go on. It didn't bother me. Our chances of getting him in the next couple were plenty good, and like I said, a nod over a guy with his class would be plenty good enough for tomorrow's angling.

"Work on the right one, Johnny. We're O.K., doin' good."

The bell rang. Johnny hooked at the eye a couple of times and just about closed it. He landed a straight right to the head that bounced Patrick into the ropes, and followed it with a half dozen solid shots at the body. He had him going for sure. Then he stopped; he just stood there and looked at Patrick twisting and turning on the ropes like he was still being hit. Patrick kind of staggered into a clinch and was holding on like crazy. Johnny wasn't even trying to work free. He looked at the ref, like he thought he ought to do something about it, but that was all. The ref broke them for a minute, but Patrick fell right back in. Who the hell could blame him? Only one I could blame was Johnny, just letting the guy ease his way back into the picture when he should've been in dreamland.

With about thirty seconds left in the round Patrick shook his head clear and they was going at it like before. He was still moving kind of flat and just throwing the left wild. Then it landed! Just like that afternoon in with Lenny, Johnny dropped his guard. The wild left hook came in and landed on the button. Johnny went tumbling all over himself, landing in Patrick's corner. The crowd yelled like you thought it was the Yankee Stadium. Patrick was so groggy by now it was tough for him finding a neutral corner and dragging himself over to it. Lucky thing for us, giving Johnny a couple extra seconds. He pulled himself up on his elbows with the ref hitting "six." He was on one knee and shaking his head clear at "eight." Right on "nine" he came up all the way. The rest of the round they fell over each other, it being tough to tell who was more beat. When Johnny came back to the corner he looked O.K.

"You with it, kid?"

"Sure, I'm fine."

"They ain't gonna stop it now, you can be sure of that. You're way ahead, there ain't no doubt about it, but it ain't nothin' to count on up here. You got to go all the way this last one. Got to take him out, if you can. Throw the right all over the place."

It was no use bawling him out now about letting the guy off the hook. That was for later.

He didn't go all the way in the next round. Just kept hacking away at the eyes, missing most of the time. He sure didn't look like Billy Graham any more. I thought now I was most likely kidding myself in the first place.

When they came back to their corners, the crowd gave them both a hell of a hand, more for Patrick, him being the home towner. Johnny sat down on the stool, still strong as hell.

"You got plenty left. Why the hell didn't you go like I told you?"

I threw his robe over him.

"They'll give it to us," Johnny said.

"Yeah? That little tumble may count for more than you think. They won't need much excuse to—"

The bell clanged. The noise went down. The announcer started reading from the slips in his hand:

"Judge Hank Gilmore votes six rounds to three, one even, in favor of London."

Patrick put both arms over his head and made like he was tossing garbage or something in the way of Gilmore. It was like about four out of five there was booing their heads off.

"It wasn't that close, not nearly. What the hell are they booing for? Is he kidding with that act over there?"

"All they remember is you rollin' around in the rosin. You was the one that went down, remember?"

"Yeah, but that was just one… "

"Judge Clem O'Hara votes five rounds to four, one even, in favor of Patrick."

I thought they was going to tear the place apart they was so glad of that one. Johnny didn't do a thing. Just looked at the announcer like he expected him to take another look at the slip and see he read it wrong and tell us about it. He read it right. Never yet knew one of them to read one wrong.

"Ben, what the hell's happening? How could… "

"Seems like some people here ain't too sore about it. What do you want me to do? I told you it could happen here. It hasn't yet, but… "

"Referee George Waxman votes six rounds to four, favor of Patrick. The winner, on a split… "

You couldn't hear any more of it for the noise. Patrick was jumping all over the ring like a kid. He ran over and pounded Johnny on the back and went on about his jumping. Johnny smiled at him kind of funny. I wished I was up to smiling. We piled out of there and headed back for the dressing-room. A lot of

guys yelled at us as we pushed through.
"Tough break, kid."
"You'll get him next time!"
"You was robbed, Johnny."
It was easy to tell they liked him. Only thing was, Patrick was the local boy, so they went with him.
When we got back to the locker, Johnny rolled himself onto the table and Tony started working on him easy. There wasn't a mark on him, except for a little red here and there.
"Well, it happened this time, kid. It would've anyway, sooner or later."
"Whadda you mean?"
"There in the ninth when you had him goin' for real and let him get away. So, he comes back and decks you like one of 'em had to sometime. We just went back around ten months. You know that, don't you?"
"You know as well as I do, I won. When we came up you knew we might get a rough decision. You told me so."
"It shouldn'ta gone to a decision. It should've been over in nine, or sooner, if you'd got in there and belted like you used to. If you could do that and still keep the stuff you picked up since then we'd be cruisin' for sure."
"I still won."
"Yeah, well, we'll pick up a paper in a coupla hours and check it, what do you say?"
"All right, so I screwed up. I'm sorry. What do you want me to do? Don't you think I feel as bad about it as you do?"
"No. No, I don't. I think that's the trouble—part of it. I think a few months ago you woulda felt like I do. Not now."
"Oh, for Christ's sake, we'll come back O.K., Ben. It was just a fight, not a war."
That did it. I kicked the pail lying there clear across the room. I just cursed as best I knew, not in sentences, just words. Right there he'd put it the way it was now. "... just a fight, not a war." Back a while he wouldn't've thought of thinking like that, much less just coming out with it, like it was a right, kind of natural thought! Then it was war and life and the only thing that mattered. Now it was just a fight we lost on a bum decision. So, we were slowed up for a while. Nothing to worry about, no sir. Just do better next time, that was the ticket. Things will shape up, most likely. If they don't, well, maybe it'll be for the best anyhow. When you think about it, look how guys like Kid McCoy, Willie Jackson, Billy Papke, and Jack Johnson ended up. It would be

tough to do worse than that. Being champ could change you in a lot of ways, and a good chance it wouldn't be for the better. People who like you now might not like you if you change too much. That wouldn't make much difference, excepting for one person. That would make all the difference.

Maybe it wasn't war in there tonight, kid. It's war from here on, for me—and the girl. I tried to steer you, Johnny, but now I got to do it the nasty way.

I didn't want to, honest to Christ I didn't.

I went on upstairs to the lobby of the hotel, leaving Johnny and Tony down in the locker room. I was so boiling mad I didn't trust myself down there with him. I was on my way across to the elevator when I felt a hand on my arm, a soft one—Gino's.

"What's your hurry, Bengy? Having champagne upstairs for everybody?"

He laughed hard.

"Glad you can laugh. I thought you had a wad on Johnny."

"The breaks, Bengy. The way I look at it I saved myself about fifty times what I lost by not takin' the punk off your hands before like I wanted to. I can see why you ain't laughin'. You kinda lost both ways, huh? Funny how I got the idea you had somethin' there. Must be gettin' old—that maybe it?"

"I wouldn't know."

"Tell ya what, I'll buy ya a drink, Bengy. I can't let my old pal down on a bad night. That ain't Gino Martell's idea of friendship."

Gino Martell's idea of friendship would make you puke. I knew it had to be an angle, but I sure needed a drink, so I went along. We got a booth over on the side and ordered.

"Y'never know how they'll call 'em here, do ya? You guys got robbed. Only thing is, there shouldn'ta been no need for a decision. Besides, it woulda been good to be ready for it, if there was. I don't think you been spreadin' the profits around enough."

"Ain't much to show in the way of profit yet. I was in up to my neck when we started out."

"Yeah, well, there's a couple places it just don't pay to cut corners. If I had the kid, there wouldn't be no need for it."

"You tryin'a tell me you still want to move in?"

He picked a piece of pretzel out of the bowl on the table and bit off a hunk. He did it like he was doing it to keep from saying something.

"It ain't hardly like movin' in any more. Takin' him off your hands might be a little more like it, don't ya think? Before, I guess maybe we both was thinkin' maybe he was good enough to make it without any special pushin', but he ain't that good. Fact, after tonight, I ain't even sure if he's good at all. Right now, I doubt he's goin' far, even with everything stacked for him. I'm willin' to take a chance to help out an old pal, y'know?"

"Pretty swell of you, Gino."

"You bein' funny?"

"Naw."

"Don't play games with me, Bengy. I got a plane to catch, not much time. Y'wanna shoot it, play games, we do it back in the big apple when we got plenty time. Right now let's make it business."

"I gotta think on it, Gino. I'm not making any deals tonight. I'm still too sore to see straight."

"I don't blame you. The way he walked into that hook, after he shoulda been back in the shower. I was catchin' that in a couple his other goes. I said to myself then, naw, who's he kiddin'? Old Bengy's givin' him the word to hold back, don't want the world knowing what a find he's got 'fore he's ready for 'em to know. When I seen it happenin' tonight I stopped watchin' the fight a coupla seconds. Know who I was watchin'? You, Bengy. The look on your kisser was really somethin'."

"Yeah?"

"Yeah, Why be stubborn? So ya picked a lemon—we all do. I think maybe I can scrape up a little of this one. Maybe not. But I got the dough and time to fool around. You don't. I still pay a right price, show ya what a guy I am. Hackett pays off what he's in hock for and still's got enough left over to look around for another boy. See?"

"I don't know, Gino. Like I said, I want to get my head clear. I'll let you know when I get back in town."

"It ain't the way I like to do business, Bengy. The deal may not hold up that long on this end."

"That's the chance I'll take, then. Tell you something, Gino. He ain't the easiest guy in the world to work with. You'd be taking on a lot of troubles you don't even know about yet."

He grinned in a way that made me almost sick the way I was feeling. I got a pretty strong stomach, but it was wobbly now.

"Never yet found one wasn't easy to work with—when you talk 'em right. You just ain't firm enough, Bengy. Maybe that's all the straightenin' out he needs. He ain't gonna get it ever from you the way he will from me—and the boys."

I saw a twenty-year-old colored boy a couple of years back, just after Gino and the boys got through talking firm to him. He

70

was lying in an alley with his face smashed in. I noticed they didn't touch his hands, but for some reason he still never went very far. Plenty of Gino's boys did, so it didn't prove much.

"You might be one hundred percent right. I wouldn't say no. You got to let me think on it, that's all."

He got up, looking at me in a way would've scared me silly once. Why it didn't now, I don't know.

"You know where to reach me. I wouldn't sit on it too long. Do yourself and the kid a favor." Then, grinning again, and like he was sure how it was going to come off, "Even if ya decide to do it the hard way, stop by and have a drink anytime. Always a pleasure to talk over old times with one of the originals. Bring the kid along. We'll have entertainment. Kids need it, even if we old guys don't."

He winked in a way you wouldn't want to see. When he took off I felt like I was able to breathe again.

"You can't do it, Ben!"

Ruth was yelling and carrying on, giving me hell like never before. It looked like I should never've said anything about how I was planning it—not planning it, really, just the way I was going to do it.

"Don't kid yourself. I'm gonna do it. I don't want to hurt him, but there's no other way now. He won't listen to nothing I say about it any more. If he did, he wouldn't believe it, anyhow."

Ruth clenched her hands into fists and sat down on the other side of the room, like she was trying to get herself steady. It was the middle of Sunday afternoon and Johnny was out; it was easy to figure who with. There wasn't one day since the Patrick fight he wasn't with her at some time. The fight was about a week back.

"You've been drinking, Ben. You're not yourself. Let's talk about it in the morning."

"Why don't you just have one with me, kid... or have you sworn off, for real, as an example for Johnny?"

She looked at me like as if she wasn't able to believe I was saying the stuff I was.

"Who do you think you are, Ben—God? You have no right..."

"Naw, I'm just a prize fight manager, who ain't gonna let what Gino Martell calls a big talent go to waste. It's very simple."

"But it's not worth it to—"

"Now you're talking like him—yeah, I know, there are bigger things than winning fights, even getting to be champ—the hell there are! Not for us there's not, there can't be!"

"There are for me."

"Maybe one thing you forget is this is my last try. Remember, you made me promise that a while back. If I don't make it this time..."

"All right, Ben. If that's the reason you think you have to do it this way, then forget you ever made the promise."

"Not me, never forget a promise, not even little ones—'specially not this one."

"Because you don't want to."

"You think that's it? You know, you might be right. Whatever it is, that's how it is."

"You can't tell what may happen, Ben. It's too dangerous, taking him to that awful Martell man, letting him find out about that girl. She made a mistake once—can't you let her alone now? Think what Johnny might do!"

"Don't worry. He's like what you said one time—'A sensitive boy,' paints and reads and all that. It won't kill him, though. There was a big driving feel for fighting in him when I first met him. It's still there, only buried or relaxed or something. I'll be ready for anything if Johnny tries anything."

"It's just crazy. I won't let you do it."

She was looking around with big, wide open eyes, as if to find something that could keep me from it. I had a feeling if there was a gun around she would've held it on me, maybe even used it. Not for keeps, but...

"Ben, listen to me, please. Don't do it! I've never begged you for anything in my life. I'm begging you now. I don't want anything that would come of this. I don't see how you could. The man I married wouldn't have..."

"No, maybe he wouldn't, I don't know. But he was a pretty different guy. He didn't have his back against the wall. Most likely, that's the difference."

We heard a key working on the front door. It was Johnny. He came in full of fun.

"Hi, gang! Hey, what's going on here? I never saw such deadpans! Let's get with it. Why don't we go out to an early show or something."

"We didn't make plans along those lines. Didn't expect you back this soon. How do we rate?"

"Rain had a seven o'clock art class over at—oh, come on, cut it out. Let's go out and have some fun!"

"You and me's going out, kid, but not for fun."

He frowned and started to pull his coat off.

"You might as well leave it on. We're leaving right now."

"Yeah, well, what's the mystery? Where are we going?"
Ruth came over to him, taking his hand. "Johnny, don't go with him, there's no reason for you… "
I should never've told her.
"I don't get it, Ruth. What's the… "
She turned away from him to me, with her eyes saying "Please," like I never saw it before. It wasn't good to see at all.
I went into the other room and got my coat. Then I dug out an old pair of brass knuckles from the bureau. I never used them and I don't know why I kept them all those years, but I was glad then that I had. I had a feeling I might need them, in case there was the kind of trouble we were talking about before. It wasn't that I'd mind the killing, but Johnny was the last guy in the world I'd want taking the rap.

When I came back in the parlor, Johnny was running his hand through his hair saying, "Gee, Ruth, it seems like he's had a couple. I think I ought to—"

"Don't! He'll be all right. You'll both be sorry afterwards if you… "

I broke it up.

"You ready, kid?"

"Yeah, I'm ready. You sure we have to go wherever we're going?"

"Plenty sure. Let's go."

The kid picked up his coat and we started for the door. I was going to close it behind us when Ruth came running up to grab my arm.

"Ben, please let me talk to you—just one minute."

Even when she used to try to stop me from quitting work whenever I found a new fighter, I never felt her asking for it so much as she was asking me to lay off this thing. I looked at her and knew if I went back in to let her have another say about it I might be a goner. I knew what I was doing. I'd had a few drinks, sure, but it was on account of I knew what I was going to do that I had them.

"We may be up late," I said. "Don't bother sitting up for us. Why don't you go over and see Joe and Margaret, watch TV, play some cards."

"Ben, you've got… "

She was standing in the door now, so's I couldn't close it. I turned away and went down the steps.

Johnny dropped behind me a sec. I heard him saying something like, "Don't worry about him, Ruth. I'll keep an eye on him."

73

We won't get into any trouble."

She was trying to make him get it, without spilling the beans. "Johnny, you don't understand, I'm not worried about… "

He wasn't staying to hear it, but came jogging along down beside me. He put his hand easy on my arm just before we climbed in the car.

"Ben, I've never seen Ruth like this. She's plenty upset. You sure you have to leave her feeling like this?"

"I'm sure. Get in."

"You get in. I'm going to do the driving. You're in no shape to—"

"The hell I'm not. I never yet been so drunk I couldn't do it better than you."

Swinging out of the driveway, we both half-turned to look at the house. Ruth was still standing there in the doorway like she was expecting us to pull around and come back. I felt like a louse, but I knew I was going to feel worse in a little while.

We were driving off the end of the bridge on the other side before the two of us said another thing.

"Did you ever think about what a lucky guy you are, Ben, having a wife like Ruth? It's a hell of a thing when you have to make her feel like that. I sure hope you got some big reason for going wherever we are."

"I got a big reason, don't worry."

"Well, just where the hell are we going?"

"To see Gino Martell."

Johnny swung around to face me full.

"What the hell are you talking about? I told you how I felt about that guy in Boston."

"Well, ain't that tough? I suppose that means we can't talk business with him, even if he's able to do us a ton of good."

"What kind of business? Whatever it is, we don't need it. I can win my own fights—most of them."

"Yeah? Most of them, huh? Like last week?"

Johnny stared at me while I was moving crosstown over to Park Avenue. We hit Park and turned right, going uptown.

"You must be stinking," he said. "I don't know how the hell you can see to drive."

"So I got to be stinkin', 'cause maybe I'm thinking about lettin' go of my big, promising light-heavy contender? Ain't you bein' a little haughty, on the face of last Saturday's—"

"That's got nothing to do with it. I wouldn't be part of Martell's stable if it meant getting the hell out of boxing and going back to slinging hash. Only thing, it wouldn't now… "

The last he said low.

"What the hell makes you think it wouldn't? You think because you won a coupla fights, had your mug on TV once, now you can go walkin' past the college kids in grey suits into some desk-type job? You think they're gonna want you sittin' around just 'cause they might of read once in Dan Parker's column you had a fast right hand? You think they'll figure it'll make you fast at addin' and sellin' and filin' or whatever the hell they'd be lookin' for?"

"Barney Ellis is looking for a young guy to help manage the resort with him. He… well, he kind of said that if things didn't seem to be going right with us, or if I caught a couple coming in too hard and decided—you know, like you said the day I met you—there was an easier way to make a buck, he'd be glad to consider me for the job. Rain says they've got courses in that sort of thing, that you can take while you're working at it. That's what I meant."

"Why that double-crossin' sonuvabitch! I used to think Gino Martell was the worst—up to now. I thought Ellis was hintin' once he'd like a piece of you, when he saw you was coming along good. Sort of return for carryin' us on the cuff for awhile when we was starting out. Funny, I would of cut 'im in—glad to do it— if he'd come and said somethin' about it. It looks like a piece ain't enough for him now. Manage his resort! Maybe you'd do it for three weeks, or somethin'. One'd get you ten he'd find you wasn't doin' the job just as good as he figured you might. Still, he likes you, and he don't want to send you back slingin' hash—'specially if his little princess has still got her eyes on you. So, what to do? Let's think about it. You'd be pullin' on yer gloves again that same day. You'd be fightin' for dough again in a month—only under new management. It would kind of take care of that middle stuff, like buying contracts. Wait'll I tell Gino this! He ain't even an operator in Barney Ellis' class! That sunuva—"

"You're not going to tell anybody, Ben. It was on the level."

"Oh yeah?"

"Sure it was. I guess something you said to him gave him the idea maybe you were going sour on me, I don't know. He didn't say it in so many words, but that's the way it sounded. He's got to know by now that Rain and I are pretty definite about everything. He just wanted me to know it wasn't the end of the line if… "

"It sure must be great to be young and believe everything's the way it ought to be. Only thing is, it comes back and hits you in the gut even harder when you find it ain't that way."

We pulled up in front of the awning in the Eighties on Park Avenue. It started to rain when we was coming over the bridge. The doorman was down at the corner trying to get a cab for two old guys in evening clothes. If we went upstairs Johnny was most likely going to get hit in the gut harder than he ever had been in his life, maybe ever would be. All of a sudden I wondered if I had the guts to do it. Or, maybe, if I was that much of a louse. It figured to be either the best thing I ever did for him or the worst. It wasn't going to be in between.

"Let's go."

"I'll wait here. I don't want to see him."

"It won't hurt you to come up. I'm likely to be a while."

"What for? I told you I'm not fighting for him. How long's it going to take to tell him that?"

"All right, so you don't fight for him. There ain't a guy in the business can make things snap the way he wants 'em to, quicker and with less strain. We might be able to do some business anyhow."

"I'll come with you, Ben. Just because I don't think you're in great shape tonight. I told Ruth I'd look out for you. Don't blame me, though, if I get up there and insult your important pal."

"He ain't my pal, by a long shot. He can do us good, if he wants to. Why kick it away?"

"Let's get it over with."

We went through the front door and two guys about six-three in uniform stepped in front of us.

"Yeah, who y'wanna see?"

They were most likely one reason Gino picked this one particular place for his pad. Or, just as likely, he had them put on after he moved in. He took charge wherever he went.

"Mr. Martell. You can tell him Mr. Hackett and Mr. London would like to drop up, if he ain't busy."

"I'll call him. Take a seat."

The smaller of the guys went over to the wall switchboard and plugged one of the gizmos. The other went over and stood by the elevator like he was expecting us to make a break for it. I would've liked to watch his expression after Johnny tagged him once. The other one was talking low into the phone. He hung it up and turned to us, looking unhappy.

"Mr. Martell's got a few friends up, but he says it's O.K. for you to come on, anyhow—they're leavin' soon."

It was like he was real sore it was O.K. He nodded at the guy at the elevator, but like it was hurting him to do it.

Going up, the other guy looked us over like he was thinking maybe we were pulling a fast one. When we stopped, he waited a little before opening the gate. I almost thought he changed his mind about us and was going to take us back down. He slid the gate to one side.

"Here y'are."

He thumbed at the door. Gino had the whole floor. I pressed the buzzer. We could hear laughing and singing and glasses.

Gino opened up. He did it kind of slow; he had to, because he was holding a glass in one hand and this little dachshund he owned in the other. I'd forgot about the dachshund, only seen it once the other time I was up here. I swore that time I'd never be up again. It just went to show.

Gino was wearing a wild Chinese kind of bathrobe, and you could see the wilder silk pajamas he had on underneath. There was some fresh spots on them like he'd spilled his drink a couple of times, or something.

"Gentlemen, it's a pleasure. Been expectin' to hear from you before. But, better late than not at all, huh? Come on in and meet my friends. Have a coupla drinks with 'em, we'll kick 'em out and talk business. That's the ticket, huh?"

"I don't know how much business we're gonna have to talk, Gino. I still feel the same about Johnny's contract, if that's what you mean. You said to just stop by for a drink sometime. That's all we are doin'."

"Swell, swell, Bengy. Who wants to talk business tonight? I'm feelin' too good, aren't we, Arthur?"

He stroked the dachshund with three fingers, holding the glass with two. The animal stuck his wet little nose inside the folds of the bathrobe and Gino giggled and made like he was shivering.

Gino walked us around the room, introducing us and all the time holding Arthur close to him. There were seven men and eleven women. I never saw any of them before or since. There was a buffet table out with plenty of turkey and eats all over it. Most of the action was around the other table with the drinks on it. Everybody was drinking and showing it pretty much by now. Johnny and I didn't have much lunch, so we grabbed a couple of ham sandwiches and some ginger ale and sat down. The talk around us sounded like it was mostly about shows—musicals and television and stuff. Most of the girls there couldn't have been out of their teens yet. They were coming out fast. There was one little brunette, looked like she should've had her own show going on around her; she looked a little scared of everything, and Gino kept

77

following her all over the room.

Johnny and I sat there a while and Gino asked us if we didn't see any girls who struck us right. We hedged around with that one for a little but neither of us did anything about it.

Finally Gino began to shoo them out. He wanted to talk business with us, he said. Real private.

When the last one was gone and Gino came back down the hall into the room, Johnny was looking at the big painting over the mantelpiece; it seemed like it was in charge of the whole place. It was a little old dark woman in a black dress. Gino came up behind him and put his hand on his shoulder.

"Ain't it great? The light don't fall on it just right yet. I had the goddam guys in three times tryin' to show 'em just the way it's gotta be for them eyes to show up right. Ain't that some face though? There's a woman who knew what she wanted and was gonna get it, no matter what."

"What was that? I mean, what did she want?"

"For me to get a chance—to be a success, if I had it in me. She got me the chance and I guess I came through, huh?"

"She's pretty proud of you today?"

"She would be, I hope, God rest her soul, if she was alive. I think she saw I was on the way when the good Lord took her."

Gino crossed himself. Johnny looked at him like he couldn't believe it. Gino didn't pay it no mind, since he was off in the blue somewhere, thinking about the little old dame who let him get the break. He came back to earth.

"I tell you boys, I got a picture in the other room I think you'll get more of a kick out of. Since you didn't know Mama, this one can't do a thing to you, like it does to me. This other, you don't need to know the party at all. Maybe I showed it to you last time you was up, Bengy?"

"Yeah, ya did."

Gino was opening the bedroom door. Johnny was standing in position so's he couldn't help but see the picture up over the big Hollywood bed. Gino stood back to one side of the door and pointed to it.

"Now, I ask ya, in all fairness, didja ever see a job like that?"

Johnny started walking to the bedroom door, staring at it like he was in a dream—a lousy one.

The girl was naked, lying stretched across the couch that was the one in the front room. She was looking straight out from the canvas, not smiling or frowning, or anything, just looking. You wouldn't have believed there was a real-life body that good, unless you'd seen it. I had. So had Johnny. It was his girl—Rain. Gino looked at Johnny and laughed.

"Hey, get a load of the kid, Bengy! I seen guys go bug-eyed before when they first spotted it. Never like this." He turned back to Johnny, who was standing at the end of the bed, looking. "And what a dame! I remember our first time—Christ! Say, kid, maybe I can fix up an introduction—when you're one of my boys. Not that I wanna influence you one way or the other." Then he laughed like hell.

Like a shot, Johnny went at him, going for his throat. I was ready with the brass knuckles and I moved fast. As it was, Gino's face was like a beet and his eyes going to glass, when I took Johnny out with the first crack.

Four

"Outside of a busted jaw and a cracked rib and my hands busted up, I feel all right."
—Kid Broad

ONE SPORTSWRITER said, "The second London-Patrick fight put boxing back fifty years."

Only thing I know is, Johnny got born that night into everything he should have been... and a lot more.

I admit I was plenty worried beforehand, a lot more than for the first one. I knew Johnny gave the girl her walking papers, but we never talked about it. He never looked so bad in training. He wasn't eating good and his weight was down. He was tossing around in his sleep at night and he looked real tired coming down the aisle to the ring. Looking at him close then, I figured maybe this was going to be the last time it was worth it for either of us.

When the bell rang he came out slow. For the first couple minutes he was moving flat and Patrick was making him look sick. Patrick caught him with the hook cleaner even than he did in the first fight. Johnny crashed back against the ropes. He was shaking his head, with Patrick coming in to end it. Patrick gave him a right to the body and threw the left again for a bulls-eye. Johnny went down. I wouldn't have given nothing for his getting up. He was flat on his face when the ref started the count. Patrick bounced right over to his corner. He wasn't going to get no extra seconds this time. Johnny didn't move a muscle 'till "seven." Then he snapped up to his knees, like some hands you couldn't see was pulling him up by the elbows without his knowing it. He swayed there, like he might pitch over backwards, or go right down on his face again. At the end of the "nine' he lurched up, his legs wobbling. The ref wiped the rosin off his gloves, looking in his face to see if he was of this world. He stepped back and waved Patrick in for the kill. Patrick moved right in, aiming to get it over with fast. He whipped out the hook again, but Johnny was rolling with it this time. He fell against Patrick, grabbing him around the waist, holding on for life. The ref tried to break them, like the crowd was yelling for, but he couldn't budge Johnny's arms. Johnny wrestled Patrick against the ropes, then turned himself into them, pushing and pulling, so's the ref couldn't do a thing 'til he was ready. When he did yank them apart a lot of the crowd must have been able to see Johnny clear. Only the ones up close was able to see the look in his eyes. It wasn't like he was looking at the newsstand guy or at the woman in the bus. It was like the way he looked at Gino when he went for him that night. Patrick saw it. You could tell by the way he held up a second or two, not moving right back in on him the way you would have thought. He never did move in. Johnny came after him like he had him set up, instead of just having got up off the deck himself. He went to the body better and faster than he ever did before. Patrick was bobbing on the ropes when the bell rang. He dropped his hands. Johnny hit him harder than he did in any other round of fighting. It looked like he was going to shoot another one when the ref grabbed him, holding him back. The three guys came hustling out of Patrick's corner to grab their fighter, it looking like he was about to go down. All of them were cursing at Johnny and yelling at the ref to do something about his hitting Patrick after the bell. Johnny shouted something back at them, same style, and looked like he was going to go at one of them when I came jumping out after him, pulling him back to the stool.

"Gimme some water! My throat's on fire!"

His voice sounded like I never heard it before. The sound of it was cracking dry, but the big difference was the snarl in it. I could feel a thing go all through my body when I heard it. I was able to see bumps on my arms. I was able to feel them all over me.

"Stick your tongue out!"

"Gimme some... "

"Shut up! Stick your tongue out!"

He did. I wiped it easy with a wet towel.

"O.K.?"

He nodded, leaning back with Tony going over his face with a towel.

The crowd was letting Johnny have it when he started to move out for round two. Then Johnny shuffled in and started to go for the body. Patrick doubled up and Johnny started to give it to him with combinations so fast you couldn't follow. Patrick grabbed for a strand of rope to keep from going down, half turning at the same time. Johnny kept hitting, maybe a half a dozen shots on, or around, the kidneys. The ref was pulling Johnny away with Patrick sinking down, like in slow-motion. Johnny looked like he was going to go after the guy, rolling down there on the deck. The ref was screaming and yelling, going red, white, and blue. Johnny was spitting something out at him and then moving to a neutral corner, like it was the last thing he wanted to do. I never would have thought Patrick could get up. The extra seconds he got with Johnny hanging around and not going to his corner must have helped a little. He got up at "nine," a sorry-looking sight. He sure was never hit that hard before. His face told it easy. The way Johnny came back in on him I knew our troubles were over. He shoved him over into a corner and hit him with everything in the book and a few wasn't there. This time there wasn't a person in the joint but knew Patrick wasn't going to get up. He went down with a straight right, lying there in the middle of the ring with his hands over his head and one leg bent up under him, like something was happening to the nerves in it. The ref didn't count or make no signal showing he wasn't going to count. He just dropped down on his knees beside Patrick, starting to bring him around. The whole place became quiet for a little, with everybody staring at the little group around Patrick, working over him. Johnny wasn't part of it. He was back on the stool, smiling a little, and sucking an orange.

"What did I tell you? We didn't need to worry about that first round."

Patrick got up with the most rubber legs you ever saw. He started feeling his way back to his corner, a couple of his guys holding on to him all the time to keep him from falling on his face. The crowd let out a cheer, seeing he was O.K. Then they went into this big all-together yell against Johnny. Some of them started throwing peanut shells and paper and stuff. Tony was yelling back at them and waving his fist. Johnny just looked out at them. His smile got a little bigger and twisted over to one side, more a sneer. One of the judges or officials or somebody, was climbing up in the ring with us, telling Johnny it would be a good idea for him to get the hell over in Patrick's corner and act like he cared whether the kid was O.K.

"Why? was what Johnny asked.

"'Cause maybe you don't wanna get killed," the guy told him.

Johnny grinned at that. "O.K." he said. For a while after that it was pretty rough. Some of the newspapers accused Johnny of dirty fighting, and there was a whole lot of screwball telephone calls from all over the country from people who saw the fight on TV and thought it was rotten. The hell with them, I thought. Johnny felt the same way. We were fighting now—really fighting.

Two years later Johnny wasn't half so good-looking any more, but he was ten times the fighter.

There were scars over both eyes that would always be there. His nose now was a fighter's nose the way you think of it. He was ranked three in the division by Nat. There was a lot of people around, including me, figured we was ready for Price. Our next go was a couple days off at the Garden with Cherry Donovan, a big vet holding down the number two spot in the book on account of a couple good wins in Canada during the year. It figured to be the test. I was surer we could take Price than I was Donovan. I saw him go twice, but not lately. I would've gone up to Canada to catch him if I could. It always turned out he was fighting right around the time we was getting ready for a big one and I couldn't get away. I felt Johnny was ready for anybody now, so it didn't worry me.

Since the fight with Patrick, nobody came close to taking Johnny. Sure, he was knocked off his feet since then, once three times in one fight by a Puerto Rican kid who was one of the best body punchers I ever seen. Always Johnny came clawing up, tougher than before. This time, he finished him in the tenth round with fifteen seconds left. The kid's forehead was split open the round before when Johnny, holding him in a clinch, looked like it was squeezing the kid's breath away, left his feet, made you think he was on a diving board, and came against it with the top of his own head. From the sound, you knew the kid was finished. He was on the deck, with the ref at "eight," when the bell rang. This time Johnny didn't finish the kid with one punch like he could have. He started raking his body with punches 'til he was doubled up. He straightened him with an uppercut. Then, with the kid lying against the ropes with his hands at his sides, Johnny billy-goated him again. So much blood came out of his forehead he couldn't see a thing. But Johnny wouldn't put him away. Why the ref didn't stop this one I don't know. Maybe he thought if the Puerto Rican could get through the round he might have a chance of getting the nod. This, on account of his good showing in the early rounds. It would have taken a lot worse decision than the one we got in Boston that time. With about seventeen seconds left, the guy was lying there on the ropes, blind with the blood churning out of his forehead. Johnny pulled back the right, like he never could have done if the guy was anywhere near this world. He hit him so hard an old sportswriter sitting near me screamed like a woman when it landed. The Puerto Rican never fought again.

There was times before when it was tough getting Johnny out of the ring. It was lucky for us that this night the commissioner, knowing what might happen, if it was a rough one, had got extra cops put on. The place was sold out. There was no local TV. If there was one of them not yelling for Johnny's scalp it was tough to tell it.

When we got inside the door of the dressing room, the commissioner was standing there with a couple of his cronies, waiting for us.

"All right, Hackett, this does it! If you think—"

"Who the hell let you in here? I got an office if you wanna get something off your chest."

"Look, I can rule London out of fighting in this state again, right now. Don't get uppity with me!"

"Sure, you can. The best drawing card boxing's had in thirty years—rule him right outa the state. That ain't gonna make a lot of people happy—people, I mean, who like to keep happy. Go ahead, take a chance on it, if it'll make you feel big. I think we'll be able to find one or two places'll have us. Got a pretty good offer just the other day from a guy in Philly, said he'd offer us—"

"Listen to that crowd, Hackett." They was still going at it outside, sounding like they was just getting started. "Don't you realize I've been warning you for your own sake to take it easy? That fight tonight was a disgrace. There was no excuse for butting that boy the way you did, London. What the hell gets into you? You were the better man, anybody could see that. You could have beaten him fair and square. You didn't need to resort to those tactics."

"Maybe you missed him hitting me low in the second?"

"No, I didn't miss it. Neither did the ref. He warned him about it. So, of course, that meant, from there on in, you had to give him the whole business—elbows, laces, the works?"

"You didn't see me complain, did you?"

"You complain? That would be really funny."

"I'm not asking for anything. I'm not giving anything either."

"Whatever the hell that means."

"It means I'm just in there to fight. So's he. If people want to make rules about it, let them. They don't bother me. I know what my job is and I do it."

For most of Johnny's fights since the second one with Patrick in Boston we'd been working in a gym uptown on the west side. When we got back to town after that fight there was a letter waiting for me from Barney Ellis. It was short. It said he figured it would be better if we found someplace else to work. It said we could settle up what we owed, or not, by check. The point seemed to be he didn't care as long as he didn't see us again. I sent him a check with no letter, paying him what we owed, and some more. It looked like now we was on the way to being able to throw it around a little. The gym was easy to get to. After Johnny won a couple more we were able to dump the crummy place we had in Long Island City and move into a swell big apartment house in Westchester. We figured it made sense to wait until we was really in the big money before we got us a house we wanted to stay with. Johnny moved with us, of course. And we didn't need to use Joe's car any more, having gotten this year's model of the same kind for ourselves. Joe and Margaret were doing O.K., too, with the share Joe was getting of the gravy for helping us get started. He was real pleased with what I decided was a fair piece for him.

One day Johnny had just finished giving a boy named Barnes a real rough going over at this west side gym. He gave it to him so that one side of his face was swollen up real bad. Johnny was pulling on his bathrobe when I noticed Old Sandy Layne coming over with a sportswriter, from where they were watching the workout in one corner of the gym. Sandy ain't really old. Thing was he retired when he was still young and middleweight champion, so people think of him as older than he is.

"Well, what d'ya think of the new terror, Sandy?" the writer asked him.

"You're good, son, plenty good. You're gonna make it, if these eyes can still see anythin'. Can I give you a piece of advice?"

"Sure."

"You don't need to leave a sparring partner in that bad shape. When you see his face coming apart like that, lay off it and work on something else. I know what you feel when you see it happening. I used to feel it myself, but, if you work on it, you can—"

"That was you, not me."

"That's right."

"So, why try to tell me what to do? I have a manager. What may have gone back there with a lot of overrated—"

"Don't talk to me that way, son. I asked you if I could give you some advice. I thought I could help you out. I thought you were a smart boy. I guess Ben here can teach anybody to look like they got half a brain. Let's get out of here, George."

"I know enough to make you look stupid the best night you ever saw."

By now there were a bunch of guys ganging around, listening in. I didn't like it. A lot of them joined in with Sandy when he gave Johnny a big "hah-hah" on the last crack. There was nobody ever fought could have made Sandy look stupid. He always looked good, even losing. Sandy's smile went off after eyeing Johnny a little more. He said, "Maybe you'd like to try it—right now."

The reporter named George took him by the arm.

"C'mon, Sandy, don't pay attention to the kid. He's just been coming along a little too fast for his own good. He don't mean—"

"The hell I don't. I'm getting tired of these old guys coming around, thinking they know it all."

Sandy turned to Al, the guy in charge of lockers and gear. "Can you fix me up with my size, Al? Sneaks is the big thing, size nine? If you're even close on the rest, it's O.K."

"Mr. Layne, everybody here knows you were the best, when you were in shape. It was a long time ago. You ain't seen any action in—"

"That's where you're wrong, Al. I guess you weren't reading the papers last year, when I was doing exhibitions for the boys in Japan. Me and Doug Potter showed 'em plenty of tricks they never even heard of. We let some of them get in there with us. They got some bang out of it! Of course, we layed off and didn't—"

"Yeah, no kidding? Real big of you! Well, don't bother laying off with me. I think I'll be able to take it."

Sandy looked at Johnny smirking.

"I won't." He started upstairs to the lockers, with Al behind him.

I took Johnny over to one side of the room, away from everybody. "What are ya trying to do? We can't get anything good outa this. Suppose you land a couple of hard ones on him, what's it prove? He's an old guy, had his best days almost thirty years ago. Maybe he can still move fast enough so's to make you look non-great. That's swell, huh?"

"Don't worry about that—not for a minute."

There was a hell of a crowd around the ring when Sandy came from downstairs. It looked like word had spread to the boys outside on the sidewalk there was going to be doings they wouldn't want to miss. You could see a mumble go around the place about what good shape Sandy looked to be in, real lean and hard. People was yelling good stuff to him from all over the place. It was for sure I was going to be the only one in there not pulling for him to give Johnny a lesson he wouldn't forget soon.

Then they were up in the ring and going at it. Eyes were bulging all over the place with the way Sandy could still move. The way you'd think he was caught sure but then you'd see he was rolling with the punch and putting in his counter; it was a pleasure to watch. At least, it would have been, if it wasn't Johnny in there with him. The way Sandy used his elbows in blocking them was a whole game in itself. With a couple of seconds left in the round, Johnny threw a right that Sandy slipped. His counter brought a look on Johnny's face that showed the old guy was still able to hit. It was the first time I ever heard anybody cheer in there.

When Johnny came back to the corner, I told him, "He was one of the best counterpunchers ever lived. Wait him out."

He tried it at the start of the next round. When Sandy got what he was doing, he did the leading. He was still in the driver's seat. I remembered once hearing somebody say that they thought Jack Johnson, when he was forty-eight, still would've had a good chance at the title, if he could have got the match. I forget who said it, but I remembered thinking it sounded real dumb. I wasn't so sure now, watching Sandy. His hands were moving faster than I would have thought anybody's could at that age. At the end of the second round he was firing combinations at Johnny's head so fast I was plenty scared. When Johnny came back this time, his nose was a little bloodied and his belly was getting pretty red. Now half the crowd there was cheering and the other half was laughing.

In the next round, Sandy was jabbing him to pieces, and every once in a while he'd step back and say something like, "You had enough, son? Here's how we used to do it!"

In would come another jab, making Johnny see what Sandy meant. Maybe two minutes of that round was gone when Johnny fell into a clinch right over me. A bunch of the guys watching yelled for Sandy to deck him, figuring Johnny was clinching because he was done. They were wrong. Johnny brought his knee up hard. Sandy's face went white, sweat breaking all over his forehead, a lot more than was there already. His hands came down. Johnny shot a left hook and a right. Sandy went down on his back. He lay there, writhing and squirming, holding where Johnny hit him low. Eight or nine people came jumping into the ring to help him. The way them guys, most of them in the business, was looking at Johnny made me feel a lot less easy than any other crowd ever did. There were no cops here, either. Right then, I don't know if I'd have tried to do anything about it even if some of them did try to get him. I'd learned a lot from watching and talking to Sandy in the past. He was always one of my favorites. It wasn't right he should be lying there now, feeling the way he was. Still, he should have known better.

"We better get outa here," I told Johnny as he was coming down out of the ring.

George, the sportswriter came over to us. "Yeah, that's gonna make a swell column. I can see my lead now: 'Johnny London, the new Mephistopheles of the ring, yesterday added a chapter to a legend of brutality and horror hitherto un–' "

"What did he expect? That he was going to make me look silly up there, that just because he had a few years on me I was going to hold back? It would've been all right. I wouldn't've minded until he started to make the cracks, playing for laughs. What was I supposed to do, just take it?"

"No, London, I don't think you could ever take anything."

Johnny sneered at that. "You're right, Ben, it's time we were getting out of here," he said. "I can't take the smell any more."

We was starting out when we heard Sandy call, "London, wait a minute!"

It was a strange kind of yell, like he had to fight to get it out. He was leaning on Al and another guy who were helping him away from the ring. Johnny and I held up, while they got him over to us. He came right up to Johnny, looking him in the eye.

"I was right," he said. "You're going to make it. You said before I should have stayed around and defended my title. I pray to God that's what you do. I'm going to see every bout you fight for the rest of your life. Then I'll be on hand the night you're reaching for it and it's not there, the night you're thinking about what to do, while the other guy just does it. It'll be a night worth waiting for."

"You gave me a little advice before. Can I give you some now?"

"Sure."

"Just keep working out with the boys in Japan. You're outa the pros now."

He went off to get dressed. I told Sandy, "I'm sorry. It was my fault. I shouldn't have let the two of you get in there. The kid just can't hold back at all."

"Don't worry about it, Ben. I'm O.K., I think. I brought the thing on. He's going to make you a lot of dough, but I'm afraid the only way I can see it ending up is—bad. I once had some of the feelings he has, but not that much. Sure, you're going to stick with him. You couldn't do anything else. I feel sorry for you, Ben."

When we got back to the apartment Johnny changed, like he did every time. Ruth was expecting us around then. She had tea and sandwiches waiting for us. As soon as we walked in, it was like he switched in to somebody else. Right away he seemed to settle down and quit thinking and talking about fighting. Instead, he'd be sitting down talking with Ruth about what she did and saw and read that day. If she got him to talking about himself, he wouldn't say anything about what went on in the gym that day, or any other, or about who he'd like to be fighting next. He'd be telling her how the country looked going up or down the drive, or about some thing he read lately. Sometimes, when he was just sitting around easy like that, I got scared maybe he wasn't going to change back when we got out. He always did. There'd be some day when he was loose going down to the gym, he'd start working kind of easy and slow, but all he needed—ever—was to get hit and he was away and fighting like he knew how.

  Ruth and I were the only people he saw to talk to at all during that time. I didn't try and make it that way. It's just the way it was. It seemed like it was the way he wanted it. Once in a while we'd go to a movie, all three of us together, but mostly we just came home, sitting around sometimes for a little gin or poker, taking it easy. It was like all that time we were waiting for his next fight that was going to bring us closer to where we were going. When we were away from home it was like he couldn't take the waiting much more, but once we got there, with Ruth around, he just seemed to go loose, as if it didn't matter if our next go was a couple of weeks off or a couple of months. I had something of the same feeling. I guess I had more of it when I first met her. It was newer, so I guess I noticed it more then.

  I never had one idea during the two years, at no time, that what happened, or anything like it, ever could. I never did find out if it happened fast, or if it was going on a while before…

  I was leaving for Miami that night. I got a wire from there the day before, asking me to come down, expenses paid, to see if a deal couldn't be worked out for Johnny to fight Price there for the title if he took Donovan that week. I was glad to see somebody else liked Johnny's chances. I left him off at the apartment around six that night, after finishing working out. I told him I'd be back the next day or the day after, for him to take it easy, and give my love to Ruth. Before pulling off I watched him stride down the walk to the front door. He was never in better shape. Donovan might be tough, but I had a few aces stowed away I didn't figure he'd be looking for. If Johnny threw them in at the right time—I'd tell him when that was—we were going to be O.K. I put her into first and headed through the rain for the Jersey airport, feeling good.

  It seems the storm got a lot worse and they had cancelled all flights by the time I got there. Next day, maybe, they told me.

When I got back to New York it was about the time we usually went out to eat, so I figured nobody would be home. I made myself a little soup and opened up a can of stew. After eating, I found I was more tired than I thought. I went into the bedroom and closed the door, flopping down on the bed. I thought I'd grab a couple of winks, but it must have been a lot more. When I woke up it was real dark. I heard Ruth and Johnny laughing loud out in the front room. I thought, when I heard it, that it was the first time since he ditched the girl that I heard him laugh hard. I was still so tired I just lay there, sort of half listening to the sounds from the other room. Suddenly, the words began to come through to me. I tried to push them away, but they wouldn't go. It was no dream.

"Johnny, please, not tonight... with the fight so close, it won't be..."

Nothing for a while but sounds. Then Ruth saying, husky-like, "It's so good when we can be—like this. You like it when it's like this, don't you?"

"How do I answer that without making it sound phony?"

"Just say 'yes'."

"Yes, more than I'm going to make you believe."

"How much? Really, Johnny... how much?"

"What do you mean? Enough so that we're here like this. Isn't that enough?"

"Is it for you?"

"Sure, it is. No it's not, but it has to be. I thought we figured all that out before. Unless you feel like having Ben..."

"I know, I'm sorry... Do you miss her awfully?"

"I thought we weren't..."

"I'm sorry. I keep forgetting, or wanting to know too much to not forget, or something. I don't really want to know."

"Good. Then we won't talk about it."

"Oh, God, Johnny—"

I had a crazy hope, being still groggy with sleep, that maybe I hadn't heard some of the words, or got the wrong meaning out of them. I didn't. When I came in, their clothes were all over the middle of the room. They were both lying on the couch.

I think if there was a gun in the house I would've killed them both—and then most likely let myself have it. The looks of feeling guilty and sorry for me, at the same time, that came on their faces made me feel like puking.

None of us said a thing. I let the picture burn in a little and then got out.

I never thought I could drink so much.

I don't remember hardly anything from the time I saw the two of them together until that Friday night. When I woke up I was aching more than I ever did since I quit fighting. There was a million little aches all through my body, and one real sharp one booting across my head, over the eyes. A lot of the things were coming back to me from those days, I couldn't figure out which was real and which was dreaming. There wasn't time for all of it to have happened.

There was a couple of cops pulling me out of an alley somewhere, and slapping me around, not hard, but friendly, trying to get me to shape up.

There was coming sober every once in a while and listening to the two of them laughing and talking, and then seeing them like that, and not being able to drink enough, fast enough to get them away. There were bartenders and more cops, trying to help out, getting sore, sometimes getting rough, usually just yelling, or doing things pretty gentle.

There was the knowing, when I woke up in the dingy Sixth Avenue hotel room, that I'd stayed in a lot better shape over the years than I figured, by the fact of being able to move. I was dressed, except for my shoes, coat, and tie. I splashed a little water on my face first and started to put them on. My hands were shaking pretty bad, but I made it with a little fumbling around. I walked down one flight and out past the desk onto Sixth Avenue. I didn't remember paying, but I knew damn well I must have. In that kind of place you always do. I headed for the first bar I saw.

It wasn't until I had a couple of jolts that I got what was going on and what night it was. I was way down at the end of the bar. There was so much noise going on, I didn't notice before. Up there on the TV screen at the other end, London and Donovan were fighting it out for a crack at Price's title. I found it tough to believe what I saw, or what I was hearing.

Johnny was getting his. One look at his face told you the ref would have stopped it long ago, it if wasn't such a big fight. It was a lucky thing they didn't have color TV yet. In black and white, you could still see plenty of blood. It all looked to be Johnny's. I ordered another drink, leaning forward to watch. When the bell rang, the announcer said it was the end of twelve and wondered what was "holding London up?" They put the camera into his corner. Tony was working there, with a couple of boys I didn't know. They seemed to know their business, but it was going to take more than that, it looked like, to keep Johnny up much longer.

I asked the guy next to me, "What's been happening?"

"It's been like this from the first round. London came out real slow, lookin' sloppy as hell. Donovan tagged him, knocked him down so fast I thought it must be a tank job. I never saw anything like it! He just stands there, leaning against the ropes, taking everything Donovan can hit him with—and then comes back fighting! I never seen a guy so game!"

When the thirteenth started, the whole bar, almost to a man, with the women joining in maybe loudest, was shouting for Johnny. Every one of them, I would have bet, came in here hoping to see him get his brains beat out. Now they was yelling for him, like he was some kind of hero or their kid brother or sweetheart or something. He was showing them the kind of guts they wished they had. None of them knew before what Johnny would be like when he was getting the business, because he never had. They most likely hoped he'd end up on one knee, whining and crying, taking the count, so's he wouldn't get hit any more. They knew different now.

Johnny got through the thirteenth and fourteenth. He was down in each one of them, but he came up swinging, even made Donovan's knees sag once when he caught him coming in. It would have put him down for keeps, if Johnny had any strength left. He'd lost too much blood and taken too many shots. Donovan shook it off and came back to clubbing him.

When the fifteenth started, everybody was rooting for Johnny to last. Would he try and back peddle or tie Donovan up in a clinch to get some extra seconds? Not on your life! Just stood there, slugging toe-to-toe with him as long as he could hold himself up and then fell back against the ropes, fighting back from there as best as he was able.

It was my voice. I could hear it. "Some hooks, Johnny! Throw some lefts! He ain't looking for… "

The fight was over. He'd lasted and half the people in the bar was standing up, along with what sounded like everyone of them in the Garden, cheering and clapping for Johnny. They was announcing Donovan the winner, but you could hardly hear it, for the cheering Johnny was getting.

I left fast. I checked my wallet to be sure I had enough to pay the fare and, seeing there was just that, waved for a cab.

"The Garden; make it snappy."

"You're too late, fella, the fight's all over. A lot of folks found out they was all wet about that London kid. He lost, but, Christ, can he take it! Talk about Ambers or Ross, he—"

"Yeah, I know. I got business there, anyhow. Step on it, huh?"

When I got down to Johnny's dressing-room, the door was shut, and a bunch of reporters and other guys was trying to push past Tony and the handlers who were working in his corner. I started to push past them.

Tony grabbed me. "Where were ya, Mr. Hackett? What a night to pick… " He stopped, looking at me real funny, when he smelt the booze on my breath.

"Lemme in, I gotta see him. Why the hell aren't you in there… "
I tried the door. It was locked.
He said he wanted to be alone for a coupla minutes."
"Gimme the key!"

He'd been taking orders from me so long, he did it automatic. I went in and locked the door behind me. Johnny wasn't in the room. I could hear the shower running. Under it was a steady thumping and a moaning. I ran to the shower room. Johnny was standing there with the hot water tearing into his body full-blast! He was pounding one fist and then the other into the wall of the shower as hard as he could. If they wasn't broken yet I figured he'd be lucky. I grabbed him and dragged him out. He tried to pull away to get back in, but he was too weak.

"Let me go… what do you care what… "
"Shut up, don't be a sap!"

I put my arm around his steaming, blistering shoulders. He started bawling for real.

"I'm sorry, Ben… we didn't know what we… "

"There's only one thing matters now, remember it—that's getting there. We ain't talking or thinking about nothing else. Lemme see them hands."

Five

"You always hurt if you're in that ring."
—Harry Willis

WE WERE beginning to think we'd never get a shot at the title. It took Donovan a year after he beat Johnny to get Price to put it on the line for him. Price was fighting exhibition matches with bums nobody ever heard of all around the country. Every once in a while he'd shoot down to South America to fight some guy you heard less of. At last, all the commissions got together, for one of their few times, and told him he was going to have to get in there with a real challenger or let go the title.

I didn't even let Johnny work out for two months after he fought Donovan. Since then, he'd been taking on everybody and racking them up. He even took out a couple of heavies was up there in the first five. Since the Donovan fight the crowds came to see Johnny the way they did before. Now it was 'cause they loved him, instead of hating him. They knew he could take it. So what, if he was a little rougher than most of the other boys once in a while? Wasn't that 'cause he was a real fighting man, who only wanted to fight? Sure it was! No fancy Dan, he. That was the way they saw it now. When you've been around as long as me you stop trying to figure which way they'll go.

The Donovan-Price go was set for six weeks off. It was beginning to look like it might be the first time the Stadium was ever sold out for a light-heavy match. Johnny and I were sitting around my room one night in the West Fifty-Ninth Street hotel we were both living in now. Johnny's room was on the floor below. Ruth was living with Joe and Margaret. I didn't see her since that night. I don't know about Johnny. I didn't ask him. I sent her some dough each week.

We were talking over how long it would most likely take to get the winner of the fight in with us. What with taxes, the winner might not be able to afford another big gate for over a year, even if he wasn't worrying about taking us on. Chances are, either one of them was thinking they could handle us, after the going over Donovan gave Johnny, even if Johnny did look good in a couple of starts since then. We were sitting around, gabbing about it when the music we had on the radio, soft, went off, with the announcer cutting in.

"We interrupt this program to bring you a special bulletin from our news room. Cherry Donovan, top contender for the light-heavyweight championship of the world, will probably not meet Dixie Price in their scheduled June 15th fifteen-round championship bout for the title. The mother of a twelve-year-old girl went to police early today to accuse Donovan of assaulting her daughter twice Sunday afternoon. Police arrested Donovan a half-hour ago in a Greenwich Village night club, where he was sitting in with the jazz band, playing the tap drums. An unconfirmed report says that Donovan has already confessed to the crime. Further developments will be reported as soon as they come in. We now return you..."

We sat looking at each other. Johnny broke it.

"How could he, Ben... with his big chance right around the corner?"

"He was a crazy kinda guy, who never knew what he was going to do. His manager did a hell of a job shuttin' up half the scrapes he got into with a fast buck here and there at the right time. Most likely, the mother woulda been plenty glad to keep her mouth shut for a coupla C's, if she only knew they was to be had. They maybe still can fix things up. They'll be able to go plenty high this time."

"It couldn't be a frame, or anything like that?"

"With Donovan in it, the chances ain't good—'fact, I'd say they wasn't there."

The phone rang. It was Casey Weiss who, being promoter of what had looked like the most money-making light-heavy go ever, now was out of a large package. Anyhow, so it might look to someone wasn't looking close, or didn't know Case better than that.

"Ben, what shape's yer boy in? Never mind, it don't matter! Will he fill for Donovan on the fifteenth?"

"We might, for the right figure." I could hardly hold the phone. I would've shot everything we'd put aside up to then to get Price into the ring with Johnny. "But, what makes ya think Price and the rest of them'll go along with it?"

"Don't worry. They will."

Then I heard some talk going on, like you hear when there's a hand over the bottom of the phone. Then on came Andy Boyle, Price's manager. There was talk Gino Martell had a piece of him now, but I didn't check it—yet.

"You boys really want a crack at us, Hackett?"

"Maybe. What makes you think they can't spring Donovan? He's been in tighter holes than that."

"He was crocked when they grabbed him outa that joint in the Village. He was braggin' about what he did, tellin' how it was and where—the whole damn thing, so's there was no doubt they had the right guy. He signed a paper, too; I got it from a contact down at headquarters. Naw, he's cooked. Look, Ben, nobody here's feelin' too great, so let's not be cute. Do ya wanna fill the spot, or not? There are plenty other guys waitin'... "

"Don't give me that! There's only one other guy in the division they'll put their mitts in their pockets to see in there with Price—that's Johnny. Try and pull the thing off at the Stadium with anybody else and you'll be givin' back every ticket you've sold. They'd stink the place out."

"O.K., Ben. We'll come around. Case'll see ya sometime tomorrow. But don't try and knock us up too high."

I don't think any of us who was in at the signing for Johnny to fight Price in place of Donovan had even a small idea of what was going to happen when the papers broke it. I guess most of us figured there'd be a few wanting their money back and the sales would slack off a little. The fact was, Donovan, who now didn't figure to be having much fun for at least twelve years, had given Johnny a hell of a beating. He didn't put him down for the count. He did everything else but, and Johnny and I was the only ones knew Johnny had outside troubles working against him that night. A few papers mentioned I wasn't in his corner, but none of them thought to make any more of it.

But when it came out that Johnny was taking Donovan's place, the rush for tickets just about doubled. All of a sudden, it began to look like the fight was not only going to have the biggest gate for a light-heavy go, but maybe there was going to be a new all-time Stadium record. They've had some big ones, too. If anyone asked for their money back, nobody heard about it.

When we started out across the grass to the ring that night, there were more people than I had ever seen all together at one time in my life. When we came out from under the stands into sight the yell was like to make you deaf. They was yelling for Johnny like he was Lindbergh or MacArthur or somebody—only with a right hand. There was maybe fifty cops around us, fighting them off. Now, it wasn't because they was after him. They loved him. They wanted to touch him, to kiss him, to grab a piece of him—a shoelace, a piece of robe, a towel he used—anything. I think maybe I was more scared that night than I was the nights they only wanted to string us up.

I guess he was to them a lot of what they wanted to be, and their kids to be—maybe everything. They knew he could give it and take it, that he wouldn't be beat until he couldn't feel it any more.

When we were starting in the ring, there was already a lot of the old champs up there taking bows. It's the custom for the old champs to go over to both corners and mitt each boy, even if he's got his dough riding against him. Every one of them fell in line, excepting one—Sandy Layne. He got the biggest hand of all. He waved to the crowd and skipped over to Price's corner, giving him the big, warm, two-hand shake. He was whispering a couple of words of advice in his ear, too, and then starting to climb down out of the ring. Johnny and I were standing in the middle of the ring. Johnny took a couple of quick steps across to where Sandy was just going to step down into the first press row. He took him friendly by one arm and asked him to come back. Sandy looked at him like he didn't get it.

"What's the idea, London? You know where you stand with me."

"Sure I do. I don't blame you. I'm sorry... that's all. I wanted you to know. Didn't you see what you were waiting for in the Donovan fight? It's not going to happen again. I was hoping you wouldn't be looking for it."

Sandy looked at me like he was hoping I'd come up with something would make it clear for him. I didn't. Sandy jabbed him friendly in the ribs.

"It's something like the way it happened to me, kid. You're O.K. You're going to come out of there with a title tonight. You don't need it, but... good luck."

"Thanks."

Sandy slid out of the ring, with Johnny looking like he got a big thing off his mind. I was glad it happened. I wasn't sure what it meant.

They had just about everyone cleared out now and the ref was calling us all over to the middle, for the usual chow-chow. Price looked in good shape. There was some stories around saying he was living too fast a life down in South America. Most likely, it was a story Gino Martell started on its way to get the odds down. Price was two pounds heavier than Johnny at the weighing-in, but he seemed a lot bigger, 'specially in the arms. They was damn near twice the size of Johnny's. You looked at Johnny's arms, you'd never guess they could do what they did. There was some bulk in Price's, close to none in Johnny's. They was a lot like Sugar Ray's, if you remember them—almost thin, when you compared them to some, with loose, flowing muscles.

The ref made it pretty short, not trying to jam up the airways, like a lot of them do for a championship. We went back to the corner, Johnny leaning on the ropes there, stretching his muscles. He looked up into the kliegs a minute, like he was praying, or something. All of a sudden, his face knotted up like something was twisting inside him or he got hit when he wasn't looking. He started swaying. I thought he was going to black out. I grabbed him by the forearms to keep him from going down.

"What's the matter? Are ya O.K.?"

He shook his head easy from side to side, leaning his whole weight against me with one shoulder. The ten-second buzzer sounded. He turned automatic, but with his eyes shut. I stepped in front of him, hearing Tony yelling at me, like from far off, to get out of the ring, so's we wouldn't lose before we started. I wasn't going to let him be standing there like that when Price came charging across after him. I shook him.

"Johnny, can you hear me?"

All of a sudden, things seemed to come clear for him. He looked at me straight. Then he looked down at Tony, yelling for me to get out of there.

"What are you doing in here, Ben? For Christ's sake, do you want to get us disqualified?"

I pushed out between the ropes, dropping down beside Tony. The bell rang.

Both guys started slow, feeling around, cozy. Price is the kind of fighter, like Gavilan, keeps his eye on the clock, pacing himself good all the time. Almost all the K.O.'s he scored, there being plenty of them, came late in the fight, after the other guy shot his wad, with him still going strong. A lot of the time, he took it pretty easy at the start and middle parts of the round, not putting on steam for real 'til the last part. It looked like it was the way they was planning this one. He was just stepping around easy, 'til there was about thirty seconds left. Then he opened up, throwing them from every direction. It didn't bother Johnny. He was rolling with them, slipping them and countering, catching them on the elbows, and at the end landed a right, had Price blinking.

The first five rounds was all pretty close. Price could be a real cutey when he wanted to. After Johnny connected with the right, he stayed low, taking care all the time to watch for it again, coming in over the jab. When Johnny came back, after the fifth, I told him to watch for the spot to toss a couple of left hooks. It looked to me like Price wasn't much worried about nothing but the right.

He was wide open for the hook when Johnny hit the target square. Price went down for nine and was lying there with the bell ringing. They brought him around pretty good between rounds. At the start of the seventh Price was trying to tie him up on the ropes when Johnny slipped on a wet spot over in Price's corner. He sat there on his caboose, gave out with a big grin, and sort of half waved to somebody out in the crowd, like to say he was O.K. Nobody there, including me, ever saw anything like it. The championship up there for grabs and he was finding fun in it! He lifted himself up easy and the crowd roared. They was loving him more than ever before. The ref was wiping the rosin off when I looked out into the crowd toward where he waved. Out there behind the press rows was the girl—Rain. She was in a white, raincoat-type coat, made her face look even whiter. It looked like there was no blood in it. Her whole face was held tight—scared. One hand was tearing into the other, like it was going to rip it to pieces.

When Johnny got up he was all business. He busted Price wide open from there in, a little more each round. The crowd was yelling louder all the time, while they watched Johnny becoming champ. It was what they came to see.

The way he was going now was like in no fight before. He was a real workman that night, more than any fighter I ever saw. He wasn't the half crazy Johnny London of the second Patrick fight and the ones after that, knowing he had to get the other guy out of there, no matter how. He was giving Price a going over, but in a way no ref was going to kick about. Still, I knew there was going to be no slowing down if he got Price in a way so's he was on his way out. All Johnny wanted that night was the championship. It was what everybody else wanted for him, except Gino Martell and a few others.

Johnny won every round easy from there in—except one. In the fourteenth Price was just back—pedaling all over, from one side of the ring to the other, trying to keep Johnny off with the jab. It showed he'd tossed in the towel, as far as having any chance of winning. He now just wanted to be on his feet at the end. Johnny kept following him steady, like a guy in a jungle on the track of something. He was coming forward all the time, with Price going backwards and sidewards, all the time throwing out the panic jab... jab... jab...

It was like all the others—light, a left jab, looking as if it hardly touched Johnny's head. But Johnny went down. He lay there on his face in the middle of the ring. The ref and Price stood there looking down at him. They figured it must have been a slip and

Johnny was going to bounce back up, maybe grinning again like last time. It was no slip.

I couldn't say nothing. Tony was screaming and crying beside me. I knew he put his whole savings on Johnny to win. That would be enough to make a lot of guys cry, but not Tony. The whole place was yelling along with him for Johnny to get up. Some of them were begging him, others ordering, and a lot in between. He didn't do it for none of them.

When the ref hit "ten," Price started jumping around all over, his hands over his head, like he'd just pulled off the biggest win of all time. He stopped quick when they started throwing things. They was throwing everything they could to get their hands on. Most of it was light stuff, but it was like the biggest hail you was ever in. They was yelling "Fix!" and hating Johnny London more than they ever did when they just had him tagged a dirty fighter.

I was down on both knees beside the doc, wondering if it could happen twice. Naw, never... not to anybody but Ben Hackett.

When the crowd saw them bringing up the stretcher for Johnny they shut up a little. The guys in white were lifting him onto it when the doc turned to me.

"Why did you let him go in there tonight?"

"What the—?"

He walked away from me to start gabbing with a couple of boys in the press who was yelling questions up at him.

You never would have thought it could be so quiet, with the crowd they had there, as when they carried Johnny out, down the aisle, across the grass of the outfield, to the street. The ambulance was waiting there. There was a mob crowding around it. The girl came busting out of it to me.

"How bad?"

"I don't know."

"Let me come along... please."

"Sure."

I guessed then—don't know why—I was wrong about her. It was too late... for anything.

There was a hospital doc and three attendants in the ambulance with us. All the way there, the doc was working hard over Johnny. He didn't move or once make a sound. They took him right to the operating room when we got there.

Just before the doc closed the door behind him he took me aside to tell me, "I'm going to try and save your fighter's life. I wish I didn't have to."

I almost went for him when he said that. Here he was a doc

supposed to be out to do good, save lives, and stuff, telling me... I didn't get it 'til three days later, when I saw Johnny again—in a straitjacket.

They had him in a separate ward of the hospital, with bars on the windows. He didn't recognize me none of the time I was with him. Most of it, he just kept staring ahead. Then, for a little, he thought he was back in Korea and was trying to figure the best spot on the hill for a machine gun. For a while it was like he was back in school and was reciting his arithmetic and things. Then he was back to just staring ahead and they was telling me I couldn't stay any longer.

I went to the office of the doc who operated on him. He said it was for keeps—"no tendency toward remission or recovery, " I think, was the words he used. He said Johnny wasn't even ever going to get to the spot where he could sell string, or anything like that. There was always going to be the chance he was going to get violent. The only thing to do was send him to a state place where they'd feed him.

"But, how... why did it happen the way it did... all of a sudden, with him not taking any hard shots that night, or nothing?"

"It was my conclusion, as I told the gentlemen of the press, when they inquired, the evening of the tragedy, that London had received a severe brain injury shortly previous to his entering the ring. X-rays taken today indicate that my conclusion was one hundred percent correct. As I understand it, no report of anything that could have caused such an injury was made to the boxing commission. You can't recall any time during his training period when any—accident occurred that might possibly have been responsible for—"

"For Christ's sake, no! Don't you think I would've had him checked over before—"

"Apparently a good many of the newspapermen don't think so. According to what I read, there was a strikingly similar case in which you were involved in the twenties. The boy was lucky enough to die that time, wasn't he? I guess there's always the chance when you postpone a fight that it will be canceled permanently, or perhaps the gate will be seriously affected. I imagine that does present quite a problem when—"

He was spitting blood and holding his face when I walked out. I grabbed a cab and got back to the hotel. I picked up the evening papers in the lobby and took them upstairs. Every one of them was still giving it the big "then-and-now" treatment, like they had for the last three days. There was reprints of all the 1925 Chicago

101

stories, along beside the story of how I sent Johnny in to get his knowing, like I must have, that he might not be in right shape. I was out of boxing for good. There was no doubt about it this time. They were going to see it didn't stop there. Maybe I could get away with that sort of thing back in Chicago, with hoods running wild all over the place. I was going to find it different here. "Manslaughter" was the rap they were going to get me on—and they were pretty sure they could make it stick. They quoted Lenny, one of Johnny's sparmates, saying Johnny collapsed one day in training a couple of weeks before, just like he did against Price. They had him saying Johnny was having headaches, getting dizzy every day since then, but I was telling him not to worry—that this fight was too big to have anything go wrong with it the last minute. Lenny and I had our falling out once in a while, but I had him figured for a good boy. I didn't hear him saying stuff like that unless they'd been working him over. Nobody was going to work me over. I wasn't giving up any five or ten years, or more, either, just so somebody could have another page in their success story.

I started packing. There wasn't much. It took about five minutes. I called the airlines and made the reservation under a phony name. I was snapping shut the bag, when I stopped and opened it again. I reached down under the shirts and got out the thirty-eight Smith & Wesson I used to carry when I was working with Joe as a payroll guard. I had a new barrel put on the frame at one of those gun stores down on Hudson Street, so's now it was just about the size of a detective special and a lot easier to lug around. I'd just kept it in the drawer, 'til I heard Gino Martell had a piece of Dixie Price. I'd been carrying it since then, not looking for trouble but wanting to be ready. I still couldn't figure why nothing had come up at all. I put it in my coat pocket. Nobody was going to keep me from catching that plane, if I could help it. The girl gave me her number the night of the fight, so's I'd call if I heard anything about Johnny before she did. She stayed there at the hospital that night and part of the next day 'til she couldn't sit up any more. She got a place at a hotel across the street. We didn't do no talking none of the time we was waiting, except for her to give me the hotel number just before she left. She said she'd be back after she got a couple of hours sleep. I didn't see her after that. I tried the number. There was no answer. Maybe she was looking at Johnny in his straitjacket now.

The lobby was empty when I got down. The first couple of days after the fight it was filled with reporters, asking me— a lot of the time sweet-like—for something to use. A lot of them was saying they wanted to help me out, see that people got my story. I wasn't falling for it. Now it looked like they'd given up.

I walked a few blocks when I got outside. Then I started moving fast, even ducking down a few alleys. When I was sure there was no one on my tail I hopped a cab. I told him to get the hell out to the airport fast. I was playing it close. I didn't want to be standing around out there waiting. My picture was in too many papers lately—every one of them, I guess.

We were shooting down Eighth Avenue, heading for the Holland Tunnel. I looked out at Stillman's and the Garden as we shot by them. Something was happening in my throat. There was the names of a couple of heavyweights on the garden marquee, guys they were playing up for a shot at the title. Johnny could have taken both of them on the same night.

When we got to the airport it was starting to rain. I paid the guy, pulled my coat up around my face. I went over to the ticket window. I gave the guy in the cage the phony name and he passed the ducat out to me. I was paying him off for it when I felt the arm on my elbow. I would have tried something but there was two of them—one on each side.

"You won't need it, Hackett."

I shoved the ducat back to the guy. He looked pretty mixed up.

One of the guys said, "We been expecting something like this, Hackett."

"I shoulda figured. Shall we go?"

"Up to you. We're going back into town. You want a lift?"

"Are you kiddin'? Ain't that the idea?"

"It was until a couple of minutes ago. We just got a call from the office. It looks like you're clear."

"What the hell are you talking about?"

"Some dame walked into the office about a half-hour ago and gave them a story that kind of leaves you out of it. She says ever since the fight was signed, this guy Gino Martell, was calling London, trying to get a little insurance on Price's winning. Seems he told him you were too old to try and wise up, but he figured London was young and smart enough to want to get with it. London told him to go to hell. I guess he didn't know much about Martell."

"He knew too much. It was my fault."

"Huh?"

"What else?"

"Seems Gino and a couple of his boys followed London and this Ellis girl to a roadhouse on Long Island one night. They came

103

up to the room London and the girl was in and tried to show him their way of thinking. London wasn't having any, so they tried to bring him around to their way—rough. She says he was out cold for twenty minutes after they left. After she woke him up by herself she wanted to get a doctor right away to look him over. He wouldn't go. He was afraid the whole thing might come out and it would hold up the fight. Maybe he was thinking of the time Graziano was talking to some gamblers and it got blowed up so big. She said she was sure he didn't tell anyone else about what happened—including you. We've been waiting a long time to get something like this on Martell. This oughta do the trick. Thing I'm wondering is, why the girl waited until three days after the fight to spill the beans?"

I could have answered that one for them. Rain knew what Martell could do—would do—if she spilled. Not only to her but to Johnny too. Then, the way I figured it, she'd seen Johnny in his straitjacket, seen his empty face, listened to his empty babbling. Nobody, not even Martell, could hurt Johnny any worse than he was right now. And me—well, I'd been pretty rotten to Rain Ellis a lot of times, but most likely she figured if there was a bigger louse than me who could take the rap, that louse was Gino Martell.

Reading the papers that night was almost funny—if you were able to look at it that way. I wasn't. Maybe in a couple of months... Most of them was saying they weren't saying the things about me they were for the last three days. Some of them were even building me up as the kind of manager was going to save boxing from the dogs—if anything could. This, by the fact of Gino's not even trying to get me to go with his plans on the fix, knowing he could count me out. There was even an official statement from the commissioner, apologizing for thinking wrong of me and saying he was going to have me as guest of honor at some big dinner, come a couple of months—the hell he was!

I was starting home with the papers when I decided to go see the girl. I thought maybe I might try to halfway square something. It would take a lot of doing. I walked the ten or twelve blocks over to her hotel. The night clerk wasn't around, so I went right up. I figured maybe they would want to keep her under wraps somewhere around the D.A.'s office for a while, so I didn't bank on seeing her. When I came to the room number she wrote on the paper that day at the hospital, there was light coming out from under the door. I was going to knock when I heard talking... a voice you couldn't never mistake once you heard it—Gino

Martell's. I leaned in close to the door.

"I guess you figured that's all there was gonna be to it, huh, baby? Just gonna have your say and the cops'd do the rest. They'd just come over and pick me up, to put into cold storage for awhile. That's the way y'thought it would be, huh?"

"Something like that."

"Yeah, well, they come over, but I wasn't there. If I thought I had a chance of beatin' this rap, I'da stuck around. It looks like ya fixed me good. I never thought you'd do nothing like that to an old friend."

"Get out of here. I'll give you one minute before I start screaming."

"Naw, honey, I ain't gettin' out—not 'til I get what I came for. Start peeling. Do it slow—like you used to in front of the mirror…"

Her voice was hard when she said, "You can go to hell."

"Look," I heard Gino say real soft, "I'm running. For the first time in my life. But not before I get what I want. Maybe I make it to Mexico, maybe I don't. But I know what I'm doing first. If y're as good as ya used to be, maybe I take you with me. If not… you better try an' make this the best ever. C'mon, sweetie, don't be…"

I heard things ripping. I put everything I had against the door and busted in. Then we were both shooting at the same time. I got in the first two. That made the difference.

He was falling and blasting through his pocket. He made a small dent in my arm. It didn't count for much. His others went through the door or into the wall. All of mine went where they were headed—five of them. He lay there, getting in the last word, with blood running all over the black pinstripes.

"Peasant!… Look what ya… done to… the suit… Three hundred bucks it cost… ya'll never… wear one… this good."

Waiting for the cops, the girl got some stuff out of the bathroom that stung when she put it on my arm.

"Can I ask you a coupla questions?"

"I can't stop you from asking."

"Why didn't you just let me take the rap, instead of blowin' the whistle on Gino—after all I did to you and Johnny?"

"I thought about it—for three days. You left a little bit of Johnny… he didn't. It was for the little bit."

We looked over at the mound under the blanket.

"How… how did you ever get… mixed up with him?"

"Pop was just starting out with the place in Jersey. He got a little tight and a little in the hole one night in a poker game with

105

Gino and 'some of the boys.' The tighter he got, the more he lost. When it was all over he owed Gino around ten thousand dollars. Pop said he'd pay him—if he gave him a little time. He didn't go to Pop, when he was tired of waiting. He came to me. He said Pop could have all the time in the world if... Otherwise, he was taking everything we had.

"Pop had worked too hard. He didn't deserve that. So, Mr. Hackett... I got with it. Does the story interest you?"

"Why didn't you tell me before? Why did you have to wait 'til—"

"It didn't make any difference. Pride, or something, I guess."

"Did Johnny know... the real story?"

"Yes. Not until after he lost the fight with Donovan. He came to me after that. He told me nothing made any difference... except being with me. He still wanted to be champ, but said it wouldn't be any good without me. Even if he didn't make it, he thought, everything would be good anyhow. I guess losing changed his values a little. He said he didn't care what I was. He wanted to marry me right away. I told him the story then. Maybe I should have told him before, I don't know. I told him I didn't want to marry him until he fought for the title. If he got to the top, I wanted to be sure he still wanted me, when, as you said, Mr. Hackett, he could have anybody."

"I'm sorry. There'll never be anything I can do to make up for..."

"No, there won't."

Leaving the station house, I thought I'd call Ruth. I was going into a cigar store when I changed my mind. I was only a few blocks from Stillman's. Ruth most likely wouldn't be home yet anyhow. I'd call later.

I started for Stillman's to begin looking for another Johnny London. I'll never find one.